One More Day

Book Three, MacLarens of Fire Mountain
Contemporary Western
Romance

SHIRLEEN DAVIES

MACLARENS *of*
FIRE MOUNTAIN
—— CONTEMPORARY ——

Books Series by Shirleen Davies

Historical Western Romances

Redemption Mountain
MacLarens of Fire Mountain Historical
MacLarens of Boundary Mountain

Romantic Suspense

Eternal Brethren Military Romantic Suspense
Peregrine Bay Romantic Suspense

Contemporary Western Romance

MacLarens of Fire Mountain Contemporary
Macklins of Whiskey Bend

The best way to stay in touch is to subscribe to my newsletter. Go to my Website *www.shirleendavies.com* and fill in your email and name in the Join My Newsletter boxes. That's it!

Avalanche Ranch Press, LLC
PO Box 12618
Prescott, AZ 86304

One More Day is a work of fiction. Names, characters, places, and incidents are either products of the author's imagination or used fictitiously. Any resemblance to actual events, locales, or persons, living or dead, is wholly coincidental.

Book design and conversions by Joseph Murray at
3rdplanetpublishing.com

Cover Design by Sweet 'n Spicy Designs

ISBN: 978-1-941786-06-2

I care about quality, so if you find something in error, please contact me via email at
shirleen@shirleendavies.com

Description

He works hard, plays hard, and always gets what he want. Now his sights are on her.

Cameron "Cam" Sinclair is smart, driven, and dedicated, with an easygoing temperament that belies his strong will and the personal ambitions he holds close. Besides his family, his job as head of IT at the MacLaren Cattle Company and his position as a Search and Rescue volunteer are all he needs to make him happy. At least that's what he thinks until he meets, and is instantly drawn to, fellow SAR volunteer, Lainey Devlin.

Lainey is compassionate, independent, and ready to break away from her manipulative and controlling fiancé. Just as her decision is made, she's called into a major search and rescue effort, where once again, her path crosses with the intriguing, and much too handsome, Cam Sinclair. But Lainey's plans are set. An opportunity to buy a flourishing preschool in northern Arizona is her chance to make a fresh start, and nothing, not even her fierce attraction to Cam Sinclair, will impede her plans.

As Lainey begins to settle into her new life, an unexpected danger arises —threats from an unknown assailant—someone who doesn't believe she belongs in Fire Mountain. The more Lainey begins to love her new home, the greater the danger becomes. Can she accept the help and protection Cam offers while ignoring her consuming desire for him?

Even if Lainey accepts her attraction to Cam, will he ever be able to come to terms with his own driving ambition and allow himself to consider a different life than the one he's always pictured? A life with the one woman who offers more than he'd ever hoped to find?

One More Day, book four in the MacLarens of Fire Mountain Contemporary Western Romance series, is a full-length novel with an HEA.

One More Day

Prologue

"Cam! We've got to move lower. Now!"

Cam Sinclair lifted his head from the unconscious man on the ground who'd been blindsided by a falling limb. The intense heat scorched Cam's face as he tried to clear his mind and concentrate. Jake Renner, the team leader, stood twenty feet up the mountain from Cam's location. He was motioning with both hands, waving toward the summit, while starting his descent.

"Wind's shifted. We have to move!" Jake watched as Cam continued to work alongside the hiker who'd been overcome with smoke while hiding in a small cave. They'd been lucky to find the man who appeared to be uninjured except for some scrapes and scratches on his arms and legs.

The hiker began to stir, choking as his eyes opened to mere slits to take in his surroundings and the two Search and Rescue workers who hovered over him.

"What the hell happened?" His voice was rough as he brought a hand up to cover his mouth for another round of deep, course choking. His other hand instinctively moved to his chest. "Damn, that hurts."

"We found you in a cave." Cam looked up to see the concern etched on Jake's face. Time was growing short.

The man choked again and tried to sit up. "I was with a group. Have you found the others?"

"Just you, so far. Can you walk?" Cam assisted the man into a sitting position and checked him once more before helping him to stand.

"Yeah, I'm good. Let's go."

Cam nodded to Jake, who began to lead the way down a narrow brush-lined trail, looking back over his shoulder every few feet.

The hiker took a step, stumbled as coughs racked his body, then tried again. Cam didn't wait any longer. He wrapped the man's arm around his shoulders, gripped him around the waist, and followed Jake.

"I'm fine," the hiker grumbled as his legs moved alongside Cam's and his grip tightened around his rescuer's shoulders.

Cam didn't respond. He was tall, over six feet, and was grateful the hiker was a slim, wiry man of average height. Cam could feel the heat at their backs and turned as flames moved down the hill toward them and their base camp. The winds had definitely shifted. He looked ahead to see Jake stopped, looking around, as if trying to find something or someone.

"What is it?"

"Thought I heard something." Jake shielded his eyes and took one more turn around before reaching for the hiker. "I'll take him. I need you to call base to let them know what's going on and that we have an injured man. My radio's dead."

Cam pulled out his radio and punched the button. "Cam to base. Cam to base."

"Go ahead Cam."

"Wind shifting toward base. Coming in with Jake and an injured hiker. Out."

"Got it. We'll be watching. Out."

Cam had stuffed the radio back into a pocket and was turning toward the trail when he heard it.

"Up here!" The voice was strained, frantic.

"You hear that?" Jake asked as he came to a stop.

Cam turned to see a slight figure in fire gear up the hill to their left, dragging someone by the collar.

"Go on ahead, Jake. I'll catch up." Cam didn't wait for a response before taking off at a sprint up the hill toward the two figures.

He came to a stop and dropped to his knees beside an injured woman. "What happened?"

"I don't know. I literally stumbled over her as I was coming down the mountain. She has a good-sized lump on the back of her head. I haven't had much chance to look at it."

Cam checked her vital signs—all seemed good. "She must have gotten pegged by a falling limb. She's not bleeding. We need to get her to base." He bent and lifted the woman into his arms before starting down the grade at a fast clip.

He'd traveled about a hundred yards when the rescuer behind him gasped then let out a shriek before falling and rolling toward him. Cam stood his ground, stopping the momentum with his legs.

"You all right?" That's when Cam got a good look at the other person—a woman.

"I think so. Pretty clumsy, huh?" She stood, stretched, then started down the hill ahead of Cam.

He wasted no time following her toward the base camp and medical assistance a couple hundred yards away. The injured woman still hadn't stirred. Cam's top priority focused on getting her the medical help she needed.

They broke ranks upon entering the camp, Cam heading toward the paramedic station and the female rescuer jogging up to a group of men near a waiting truck. He watched her for a split second before turning his attention to the open doors of the emergency vehicle.

"About time you showed up." Jake kneeled inside a waiting medical van and stretched his arms out toward Cam to take the injured woman and place her on a bed behind him. "Stay here. We need to regroup, change the base camp, and get back out to search. Tim finished checking out the male hiker. I'll send him off as soon as he looks over the woman."

Cam swung his head toward an explosion up the mountain. Fanned by scorching summer winds, the sound fell somewhere between a freight train and a jet engine just before take-off.

"Move, move, move!" The Captain of the local area's Search and Rescue, or SAR, team turned in a circle, yelling orders in all directions as everyone scrambled to clear the area. "We've got five minutes to evacuate!"

Something had ignited from the combination of strong winds, low humidity, dry conditions, and warming temperatures.

The members of Cam's SAR squad gathered in their appointed area. Jake checked off each member as the crew truck pulled to a stop.

"Load up, men," Jake called as the last member jogged up.

Cam hopped into the bed of the truck just before Jake, and took a seat at the back rubbing his grit-filled eyes. He stretched aching arms above his head and took one more look around, his eyes landing on a lone figure several yards away.

"What's going on with her?" Cam asked Jake, nodding toward the woman.

"Guess I'd better find out." Jake started to rise, only to be stopped by Cam's outstretched hand.

"I'll go." Cam was over the tailgate before Jake could object, striding toward her, while gazing around to make sure no one else would be left behind.

"Hey. Where's your crew?"

She turned, her shoulder length, jet-black hair falling over her eyes, a look of confusion, and perhaps fear, on her face. "I must have gotten the coordinates wrong. We were supposed to meet up here if anything happened."

"Look, we're the last group out and we've got to get moving. Come with us and we'll get you hooked up wherever you need to go." He took another worried look up the hill at the flames that were beginning to shift away from their location.

She stared up at him, hesitating for a split second, before nodding her head.

"Cam! You coming?"

Cam tore his gaze from the female volunteer and looked toward his team leader.

"We'd best get in the truck."

The group rode in relative silence down the mountain, watching the flames and smoke move away from them. It didn't matter, their job as search and rescue volunteers was finished in that section of the wilderness. They'd be directed to another site, another camp area where families were still focused on observing the fire that appeared to be miles away, not yet comprehending the danger it posed to them.

Cam's group, along with others from across the western United States, had arrived in the Bitterroot Mountain area of Montana to assist with search and rescue efforts. It had been a dry, hot summer and crews across the country were working overtime to keep up with the growing number of wild fires.

Cam glanced at the volunteer beside him, feeling an inexplicable pull to connect with her.

"I'm Cameron Sinclair." Cam extended his hand.

"Lainey." She clasped his hand. It was warm and welcoming, and she felt an unfamiliar, slightly uncomfortable sensation creep up her arm at the contact.

Cam smiled down at her, momentarily mesmerized by her guileless emerald green eyes and broad smile.

"How long have you been a volunteer?" Cam asked Lainey as the truck bounced over dry, rutted back trails.

"Four years. You?"

"Almost seven. Some urban rescue, although most of my experience is in mountain and wilderness rescue."

"I'd love to try urban rescue. Most of what I get is mountain, some on horseback."

"That right? I've done several searches on horseback since I moved to Arizona a few months ago. Where are you from?"

Lainey's answer was cut off as they pulled into the main camp.

"All right everyone, listen up." Jake stood as the truck came to a stop at the main staging area for all SAR groups. "Stay close. Get something to eat, take care of business, and meet me back here in thirty minutes. I'll find out our next insertion point and assignment." He looked down at Lainey. "You need any assistance finding your team?"

"No sir, I'll be fine. Thanks for the ride." Lainey vaulted over the tailgate, not wasting a minute before searching for the rest of her team. She was worried about them. They never left anyone behind, and never missed their meet location.

"Hey, wait up."

Lainey turned to see Cam come up behind her.

"Need any help? I've got time."

She looked up at his face, smudged with soot, and hidden behind reflective sunglasses that made him look cocky, and somewhat dangerous.

"Uh, no. Thanks for the offer, though. I think I see a few of them over there," she pointed toward a group several yards away. She started to turn, then looked back. "And thanks for giving me a ride." She flashed a broad smile at Cam, her eyes crinkling at the corners, before she dashed away toward her group.

"Wait. What's your last name?" Cam called after her as a truck pulled between them, cutting off his view of her retreat. He cursed softly under his breath, wondering what had come over him.

He had no time to build a relationship—at least not one requiring work, and especially not some type of long distance thing. He had plans, and they didn't include a pretty SAR worker. Cam shook his head. If he believed that, then why did he sense he'd just missed out on something important?

Chapter One

"You about ready?" It was early evening on Friday. Eric Sinclair, Cam's younger brother, had them lined up for some type of double date with a woman Eric had met at a local business meeting and the woman's partner. If Cam remembered right, they owned a CPA firm in Fire Mountain. There wasn't much he hated more than dating—any type.

He'd been on a couple of dates since returning from the last major search and rescue operation in Montana. Each time he'd tried to focus on the women, follow their stories, and enjoy the back-and-forth banter, but he couldn't stop himself from seeing a different face. The vision would come unexpected. It was of a young woman with ebony hair, fair skin, and sparkling green eyes that contained a bit of merriment as if she knew something he didn't. Her first name was Lainey, the search and rescue volunteer who'd captured him mentally during their brief encounter.

Cam had thought about her often, each time chastising himself for getting off track and fantasizing about someone he didn't know, and had no time for even if he did.

"Sure. Let's get this over with." Cam straightened the files on his desk and turned off the desk light—something he much preferred to the annoyingly bright ceiling lights.

"Look, it's just a date. Dinner, maybe some music afterwards. Besides, when was the last time you were out?"

"Last night..."

"I don't mean the company touch football game. Out on a date?"

Cam walked around to the front of his desk and leaned against the edge. "A couple of months ago."

"And was it a disaster?"

He let out an impatient breath. "No, she was great. I just didn't have any interest in seeing her again." Cam's frustration at family and friends trying to set him up, meet new women, showed in his disgusted expression.

Eric clasped a hand on his brother's shoulder. "You need to relax, get out once in a while. Look, I understand your need to succeed, follow in Dad's footsteps, and I know you have ambitions that don't include meeting the right woman. Still, you need to take a break and have some fun."

Cam wasn't surprised that Eric had pegged the situation so accurately. He'd been driven his entire life to excel, learn numerous skills, be the top at all he tried, and imitate the success his father had achieved. Kit Sinclair had been a great man and Cam's determination to be like him required complete focus and dedication.

Eric knew Cam better than anyone. Although they'd had different mothers, he, Cam, and their sister, Brooke, had always been close. Eric's mother, Annie Sinclair MacLaren, married Heath MacLaren after her first husband, Kit Sinclair, passed away. With the marriage, they'd gained a stepbrother, Trey MacLaren, a Navy pilot, and stepsister, Cassie MacLaren, a student at Arizona State. Both Cam and Eric now worked for MacLaren Cattle Company as well as the rapidly growing development division—Eric in land development and Cam as head of the IT department and as part of the company's flight team.

Cam pushed away from the desk and grabbed the cowboy hat he'd grown accustomed to wearing. "You're right. Let's get this evening started."

******

Bluebird Falls, Idaho

"Lainey, aren't you ready yet?"

She cringed at the harsh tone and inconsiderate manner of the man who stood in the doorway, leaning one shoulder against the frame while glaring down at her as she gathered up the last of the puzzle pieces the children had left behind.

"The last mother just picked up her daughter a few minutes ago. Let me finish putting things away and we can leave." She stood and walked to within a few inches of him. "Or, you can go on without me." She had no interest in spending another evening at one more of her fiancé's long and boring business dinners.

"You know I can't do that. My boss is expecting both of us. Besides, his wife is coming this time."

"Not his girlfriend?" Lainey couldn't suppress the jab. Her fiancé, Robert Crafton, was a successful attorney in a firm started by his boss, Laurence Burns, and Robert's father, years ago. Robert was now a partner, focusing on land deals and ranching operations.

"You know I hate the girlfriend situation as much as you. At least he's somewhat discreet about them."

Lainey disagreed with Robert's tacit acceptance of his boss's philandering. "Why doesn't Gladdie say something? Kick him out, move on? Geez, she's a beautiful woman, fun, more active than her husband, and wealthy. She could do a lot better than Laurence." Lainey pushed the last of the plastic bins into its cubby hole, grabbed her jacket, and slung a large, heavy tote over her shoulder.

"My guess is that it's too much work. He can have as many affairs as he wants, as long as he keeps them private. Why go to the bother of the court case, publicity, and all, when she doesn't have to." Robert watched Lainey struggle with her oversized purse but didn't reach a hand out to help her. He'd hate it if anyone saw him holding a purse.

"I'll follow you." Lainey clicked the button on her key fob and saw the back lights of her car flicker. She was due for a new one. The eight-year-old coupe had served her well and stayed alive long enough for Lainey to save up enough to pay cash for her next car. A small SUV this time, or maybe a truck. She grinned at the possibilities.

"You know I hate it when you drive that heap to business dinners. Ride with me. I'll bring you back when we're finished." Robert opened the driver's side door of his luxury sedan and slid inside, oblivious to Lainey standing on the other side, waiting for him to be a gentleman.

Robert started the car and rolled down the window. "Climb in. I'll get your door at the restaurant."

She flung her tote between them on the cream-colored, smooth leather seat, and sat down, staying as close to the open window as possible. Lainey was pretty certain Robert had consumed his usual two to three after work drinks before coming to pick her up. Vodka, if she wasn't mistaken, and some other scent that wafted past her as the cool air flowed into the car—sort of sweet, flowery.

"We'll stay at my place tonight." Robert's dictates were becoming the norm between them. It wasn't often he consulted her on their weekend plans or even asked if she had any of her own.

"I can't tonight. Remember? I've got an early morning run with my SAR team before our regional meeting."

"Your team sure is taking up a good deal of your time. Have you done any thinking about what we discussed?" Robert's stern, imperious voice grated on Lainey and she wondered for the hundredth time in the last few months why she hadn't broken off their engagement. She knew he wasn't asking a question as much as issuing a demand.

"Technically, we didn't discuss it. You asked me to consider quitting and I said no."

"You know what I mean. Between your job and SAR commitments, we have little time for each other. I can't see it getting any better once we marry."

She didn't see it getting any better, either. Lainey looked out the window at the growing darkness, wondering if tonight would be the best time to tell him of her decision.

******

"Your brother is a nice guy, Eric. Thanks so much for convincing him to come out with us." Gisele "Zell" Marlenson had been attracted to Eric from the instant they'd met at a Chamber of Commerce mixer and had hoped he'd call. She'd jumped at his suggestion of a double date as a way to get her good friend, and business partner, Megan, out of the office. Together they'd been logging way too many hours and needed a break.

"We were both looking forward to it." Eric looked over his shoulder to see Cam on his phone, frowning and nodding his head before saying a couple more words, then closing the phone and sliding it into his pocket.

Cam's eyes rose to meet Eric's. He knew his brother wouldn't like what was coming.

The last two call-outs had been during the day—one during a board meeting and the other on a Saturday in the middle of their weekly touch football game. Both times he'd had to excuse himself and leave. This would be no different.

"Apologies, everyone." Cam glanced at Megan and Zell, then shifted his gaze to Eric. "A couple of boys from a scout troop are missing in Colorado and they've called us in. I leave in an hour." He turned back to Megan. "I'd like to make this up to you another time, after this trip is over."

"I'd like that." Megan's smile was warm and genuine.

"Good. Count on it." Cam looked back to Eric. "May I take your car?"

"Sure. I'm certain Zell can give me a ride home."

Zell looked up at Cam. "No problem. Take care of yourself."

Eric dug his keys out, flipped them to Cam, then watched as his brother strode from the restaurant, certain he'd receive a text message once Cam knew where his team was headed.

******

"Dessert, Miss Devlin?"

Lainey glanced at the menu once more before handing it back to the waiter. "Nothing for me tonight."

Robert studied her, not pleased with her unusually sullen mood and lack of interest in the conversations during dinner. Lainey always ordered the restaurant's remarkable bread pudding. He knew something wasn't

15

right and would have to ask her on the trip to his place, still certain he could talk her into spending the night.

"Lainey, Laurence and I would love to have you and Robert over for dinner sometime in the near future." Gladdie's soft, dove-gray eyes crinkled at the corners when she smiled.

Lainey hesitated a moment. The odds of her and Robert still being together after this weekend were slim. "I'm certain we can work something out that will ..." Lainey stopped at the sound of her phone. She glanced at the number. "Would you excuse me a moment, Gladdie?" She walked toward the entry, not missing Robert's glare as she left the table.

"This is Lainey."

"We have a situation in Colorado. Lost Cub Scouts. They need as many teams as they can get as soon as possible. We have transportation in an hour."

"I'll be there." Lainey hung up, started back to the table, and took a deep breath, knowing this would not sit well with Robert. "I apologize, Gladdie and Laurence, but some Cub Scouts are missing in Colorado and they're calling up as many SAR teams as they can get. I need to leave to make my transportation."

She slung her purse over her shoulder and waited for Robert to rise.

"Of course you must go, Lainey. Our prayers will be with you and those children, right, Laurence?"

"Certainly. Let us know if there's anything we can do to help." Laurence took another sip of the Colheita port he

16

favored after dinner and stood. "Robert, sorry the evening must break up so soon. At least it's for a good reason." He waited until Robert took the hint and rose from his seat.

Lainey watched as a scowl contorted Robert's face. "I can call a cab if you'd rather stay."

Robert shook Laurence's hand and turned toward his fiancée. "No. I'll take you." He took her elbow and guided her to valet parking, handing his ticket to the attendant, then turned to face Lainey.

"You'll need to make a choice at some point. I don't intend to share you with your rescue team."

"Nor should you have to, Robert."

"Good. I'm glad we have an understanding."

His self-satisfied smile told Lainey her decision to break off their engagement was right. She'd make him miserable with her desire to continue in the SAR program, and Robert would eventually wring every bit of spontaneity out of her body. It would be best for both of them.

He pulled up to her place, not turning off the motor or offering to come around to help her out. They were away from knowing eyes, all need for pretense gone.

"I'll call you when I arrive." Lainey placed a quick peck on his cheek and stepped out of the car.

Robert wasted no time pulling away, his taillights dimming to nothing within a few mere seconds. She turned to watch him go feeling nothing except incredible relief.

Chapter Two

Castle Canyon, Colorado

"We have five teams," Jake announced. He'd been selected as the SAR operations manager for the search efforts to locate the missing Cub Scouts, which was unusual. The Castle Canyon SAR lead was in the hospital with a broken leg and had specifically requested that Jake take his place.

"We're searching for two eight-year-old boys who split from their den leader. The other six are back with their parents." Jake handed out flyers. "Pictures and information about each boy. They've been missing for approximately four hours. Two teams are already out and are taking positions here and here." He pointed to a map. "We'll deploy our four teams between this ridge and the river. All six teams will be taking direction from me. We expect the two will stay together. Questions?"

"Normal team leads will report to you?" The volunteer was a tall, burly man with a long reddish-brown beard.

"That's right. We'll use normal communication patterns."

"Helicopters?" A short, stocky man called from back.

"We'll have to wait for daylight. But, yes. Assuming we don't find the boys tonight, helicopters will be up at first light."

"Will medical vans remain here or be posted throughout the search area?" The group parted as an average height female volunteer came forward.

Cam watched her approach. She had a familiar gait, casual, and moved with purpose. As she came closer, Cam's breath hitched when he spotted her. She stopped next to him, not acknowledging or recognizing him.

"We have four emergency vans. They'll be located on the spots designated on your maps. No matter the condition, both boys will go for a medical checkup once found."

Cam and Lainey stood next to each other. Even after four months, Cam still felt the same incredible pull toward Lainey that he had the first time he'd seen her, covered in soot, dragging the injured hiker down the steep trail, yards ahead of the fast approaching fire.

"Anything else?" Jake asked and looked around. "All right. Time to head out."

Lainey turned back to where her team had congregated.

"Lainey. Wait."

She turned, recognition coming slowly before a broad smile split her face. "Cameron, right?"

"Cam to my friends." He returned her smile. "Look, I don't know where we'll be once the boys are found, but here's my information." He scribbled on a scrap of paper he'd pulled from a pocket. "Email me. That is, if you'd like to stay in touch."

She'd felt drawn to him during the Montana rescue mission months before and remembered her resolve to stay away from someone who triggered such intense feelings so quickly. Now he was here, a foot away, wanting to stay in touch. She reached out and took the paper.

"I'd like that."

"Good." He looked over his shoulder. "I have to leave." Cam dashed to the waiting truck as Lainey took off in the other direction. "Wait! What's your last name?" But Lainey didn't hear through the controlled chaos around them.

Lainey climbed into the waiting vehicle already filled with team members and watched Cam's truck kick up dust as it disappeared around an old mountain road. She'd known her engagement with Robert was rocky, even during her mission in Colorado, yet wasn't prepared to throw it away on some chance meeting with an unknown SAR volunteer, no matter how intense the attraction. It had been the strangest feeling she'd ever experienced. Never before had the presence of one man affected her the way being close to Cam had. It frightened as well as thrilled her.

"Lainey, you hear me?"

The deep voice pulled Lainey from her mental wandering to focus on the man beside her. Mark Hill had been a good friend for years. He'd gotten her into the SAR program in Bluebird Falls, and introduced her to Robert, in a roundabout sort of way.

"Sorry, what did you say?"

"Who's the guy?"

"What guy?"

Mark laughed—the robust, rumbling sound always made Lainey smile. "The one your eyes followed until the truck pulled out of sight. Who is he?"

"Oh, just a volunteer I met at the Montana fire. Seems like a nice guy."

"Uh-huh."

Lainey swung her head toward Mark. "What?"

"Nothing, except I've never seen that look on your face before. Not even with Robert."

"What look?" She had a hard time believing anyone could read her so well in an instant.

"The one that tells a man you're interested." Mark pulled his eyes away from Lainey to look toward their path through the dense growth and twisting trail. The sky had turned dark, leaving nothing but the partial moon, truck lights, and whatever the volunteers had available. "This is going to be interesting," he murmured before settling against the back rail and closing his eyes.

Lainey stared at Mark, her head reeling from his words. How could he possibly interpret her brief encounter with Cameron as anything more than two acquaintances talking? Was she that transparent? Apparently so.

"Almost there," her team leader called minutes before they pulled to a stop and everyone piled out. "You know the drill. Let's get going."

Lainey and Mark were always paired together. She'd met him in college and they'd become fast friends. He understood her love of children and the outdoors as well as her desire to become more involved in the community. Mark had been in the regional SAR program since his junior year and eventually broke through Lainey's initial hesitancies and concerns that she had nothing to offer. It didn't take more than two observation trips, shadowing Mark in the field, for the program to set its hooks in her.

"Have everything you need?" Mark walked up, adjusting his gear and taking note of their surroundings.

"All set." Lainey snapped her helmet in place and slipped her hands into protective gloves.

Three hours later, they'd found nothing to indicate the two boys had been anywhere near their assigned search area. The night air chilled and with it came a heightened sense of urgency. No one wanted the boys to spend a night alone in the mountains, with little protection, and nothing to ward off the cold breeze whipping through the valley.

"Base to Mark. Come in."

"Go ahead, base."

"Boys have been found. Come back to base."

"Good news. We're heading back. Over." Mark pocketed the radio as Lainey walked toward him. "They found them. We're clear to head back."

Relief washed over her. Her concern for the boys' safety increased as each hour passed without word from any of the teams.

"Thank God. Let's see how they're doing." Lainey's experience with children made her the go-to person on their team for rescues involving children. It didn't really matter if they needed her this time or not, she still wanted to see for herself how the boys had fared alone.

Base wasn't hard to find with the glaring portable lights, television crews, and over a hundred people milling about. The Scouts sat wide eyed as a doctor checked them out, finally releasing them to their parents.

Lainey watched as one set of parents then the other, each with their sons in tow, walked toward one of the SAR teams. The men cleared a path for the families who spotted the man they looked for near the back of the crowd. Lainey's heart clenched as Cam stood, shook their hands then knelt before the boys. She inched forward enough to make out some of his words.

"I can count on each of you to listen to your leader from now on, right?"

The boys nodded even though it was obvious by the slump of their shoulders that exhaustion consumed them.

"Use what happened today to make better decisions in the future and not cause your parents to worry the way they did tonight. Got that?"

"Yes, sir," each responded in low, tired voices.

"All right." Cameron grinned and extended his hand to each.

Lainey continued to move closer to the group as the parents prepared to leave.

"If there's anything we can ever do for you, please call us." One of the fathers handed Cam his card, the emotion in the man's voice thick.

"Thank you, sir. Finding the boys safe is all the thanks I need."

Lainey moved aside to let the families pass then hung around hoping for a moment to speak with Cam alone. She wasn't sure what she wanted to say—congratulate him, certainly, and perhaps give him what he'd wanted from their time in Montana, her last name and number. Doubt suddenly consumed her and she began to retrace her steps back toward her own team.

"Lainey, wait."

She turned to see Cameron trot up beside her.

"Great work, Cam." Lainey's voice washed over Cam and he had the strangest urge to pull her into his arms. He shoved his hands into his pockets and took a slight step backwards.

"Thanks. They'd found a small rock enclosure and huddled inside." He looked over her shoulder to see the families climb into their cars. "At least they had water and a couple of granola bars which they were smart enough to ration. That's more than a lot of adults do."

She chuckled, having encountered the same thing on a couple of their searches. "You handled the boys very well. Do you have a lot of experience with kids?"

"Not much. My stepbrother, Trey, has a young son, and my last girlfriend has a little girl. That's it. How about you?"

Did that mean he didn't have a girlfriend now? "Uh, I teach preschool—kids two to four years old. I love working with children—there's never a dull moment."

"No kids of your own?" He watched, fascinated at the way her face lit up when she spoke of her work and children.

"No. Someday I hope to have a family. A big one if I meet a man who loves children the way I do."

"So you're not married?"

"No, not married. I'm ..."

"Hey, Lainey. I wondered where you'd gone off to." Mark handed her a small bag filled with fruit, an energy bar, and a bottle of water. He held out another one to Cameron. "Mark Hill."

Cam grabbed the sack and shook Mark's hand. "Cameron Sinclair."

"Good work out there, Sinclair."

Cam opened the bottle of water and took a long swig. "Thanks. Luck had as much to do with it as anything."

"Luck or whatever. You found them." Mark tilted his bottle of water toward Cam in a toast then shifted his gaze to Lainey. "We're heading back, and if we're lucky, we'll be home by sunrise." He looked once more at Cam. "Nice meeting you. Have a safe flight home."

"Same to you, Mark."

Neither Lainey nor Cam budged as a thick silence settled over them, the easy banter of moments before gone.

"Well, I guess I'd better go." The hesitancy in Lainey's voice wasn't lost on Cam. "It was great to see you again. Maybe sometime in the future..." Her voice trailed off as Lainey realized her future was far from settled.

Cam stepped forward to within inches of her. "I'd like to be able to call or email you, if that's okay?"

Lainey hesitated a moment before taking a deep breath. "Look, I need to be honest with you. I'm engaged, and, well, I just don't know how things will turn out."

Cam's spirits sank with her words. "Sounds like you're not too committed to the man."

"Let's say I'm less committed to the marriage than Robert is. Even so, it wouldn't be right to muddy the waters right now." She allowed her gaze to fix on his. "I hope you understand."

He'd never been engaged, although at one point a former relationship looked like it would go in that direction. Cam had never been sure what changed his mind. He'd woken up one day to realize the woman wasn't the one. Something about Lainey made him believe it would be different with her. There was no sense to the strong pull he felt toward a woman he'd met just twice— almost like a voice inside his head taunting him with a certainty that she would be important in his life.

"You have my information. Anytime you want to reach out, just let me know." He held out his hand. "I wish you the best, Lainey."

She grasped his large, calloused hand, and the strangest sensation washed over her. There was a rightness in his touch, nothing like the cold, indifferent feel of Robert's hand in hers.

"Goodbye, Cam. I do hope we meet again sometime."

He watched her leave, once again chastising himself for his unusual and unwanted reaction to the woman. Now he had an absolute reason to push her from his mind. Even if he had the time or desire to get involved, engaged and married women were off limits. Cam took a deep breath and headed toward his group, glad he'd resolved the issue of the pretty SAR volunteer once and for all.

Chapter Three

Two weeks later, Fire Mountain

"I had a wonderful time, Cam. Thanks so much." Megan stepped out of the car in front of the house she shared with her business partner, Zell. "I'd never been to that restaurant before. It was great."

Cam escorted her up the narrow walkway to her porch. "It's one of my favorites."

She turned as they approached the front door. "Perhaps you could come over for dinner sometime. I'm a passable cook, at least according to Zell."

The evening air was cool, washing across his face, reminding him of his last meeting with Lainey. He couldn't seem to wash her image from his mind—her broad smile, enthusiasm for life, and interest in others. Cam couldn't shake his desire to have one more day with her. Just another chance to figure out if his feelings were an illusion or real.

Still, Megan's quiet, even temperament appealed to Cam. He knew she had a work ethic as strong as his and had made it clear she had little room in her life for a demanding relationship. That suited Cam just fine. Plus, they'd had a good time tonight.

"I'd like that." Cam watched a smile spread across her face.

"Great. How about next Saturday? We can invite Zell and Eric to join us if you'd like."

"Sounds good. I'll mention it to Eric and call you next week."

She stretched up on her toes to place a kiss on his cheek. "Thanks again. I had a great time."

Cam watched her disappear inside. Even though he had no interest in anything permanent, he and Megan suited each other right now.

He drove back to his home, a comfortable cabin on the ranch that Heath provided for his use. Eric had a similar setup—two bedrooms, one bath, and a full kitchen that opened into a dining area and wood paneled living room with a large rock fireplace at one end. Cozy, efficient, and private. A deck wrapped around three sides. On the rare days Cam came home early, he'd sit outside with a cup of coffee, or whiskey, and watch the sunset. It was a good life, just what he wanted.

******

One month later, Bluebird Falls, Idaho

"I know it isn't what you expected and I'm sorry if this ruins your plans." Lainey sat in the living room of Robert's large, four-bedroom home on a lake, holding tight to a cup of tea and wishing she could leave. It was a beautiful house, and with the right person, it would be a place she'd look forward to coming home to each night. Robert wasn't that person.

Robert had paced to the fireplace, putting his drink on the mantel before turning to face her, his face a mottled reddish-purple as he worked to control his anger.

"You're throwing us away because you have a sudden urge to move out of state. Do you even have a job, a place to live? Or is it you've met someone else?"

Lainey stood and clasped both hands in front of her. "I have a place to stay and a job waiting. It's something I've thought about for a long time." She reached behind her to grab her coat. "And no, there is no one else."

"Then why leave? It makes no sense." Robert could sense his protests weren't reaching through the shell Lainey had already constructed around her.

"Because we aren't meant for each other. If you think about it, you'll realize I'm not who you want. I've come to accept that we'll never make each other happy."

"What more do you want, Lainey? I'm offering you a beautiful home, memberships to any club you want, connections throughout the area, a chance to stop working, and finally quit the SAR team. We'd have a family. I just don't understand what else you could want."

Lainey listened, her expression fixed, not indicating any of the disgust she felt at his inability to comprehend her needs and what mattered to her. He knew she loved her time in SAR and had no desire to give it up. Yes, she wanted a family and felt she could balance children with work, even if part-time, and her volunteer activities. The rest, a big house, club memberships, meeting what he considered the right people, meant little to her.

Above all else, she had no desire to be controlled by a man. She'd watched her mother cower under her father's domineering rule for years—until the fire that killed them both during Lainey's senior year in college. She knew successful marriages existed, and if she were to marry, Lainey intended for it to be a partnership. That wouldn't be the case with Robert.

"That's just it. I don't want to give up working or SAR. They're both important to me. If I ever do meet the right person, he'll appreciate this and make allowances you aren't able to consider." She slung her purse over her shoulder, then noticed the ring on her left hand. Lainey slipped it off and laid it on the coffee table. "Maybe in time you'll understand this is best for both of us."

She glanced once more at Robert before walking to the door.

"Lainey, wait." He hurried to stop her before she could step outside. "Hear me out."

"No, Robert. I'm sorry if this isn't what you want, but it's what I need. Please, it's better this way." She stared up at him, her eyes devoid of emotion and lips set in a thin line, hoping he'd move aside and let her leave.

"Make sure, Lainey. If you walk out that door, I won't take you back."

She didn't hesitate. "I'm sure."

She was halfway to her car when Robert called after her. "At least tell me where you're moving."

Lainey climbed into the front seat and rolled down the window. "Arizona."

******

"We'll miss you so much. Are you sure you won't change your mind, consider staying at least through the end of the year?" Deb Dawson, the owner of the preschool had become a good friend and mentor. Lainey hated leaving her and the children, yet knew this was the right decision.

Lainey's eyes misted over as she thought of all the good times she'd shared with Deb and the kids. She'd earned a degree in childhood development, had excelled in all her classes, and interviewed at several schools before accepting Deb's offer. Book learning had helped—being on a job and implementing what she'd learned turned out to be something else entirely. She'd learned how to identify the right and wrong methods of working with children during her time with Deb, and understood the deep sense of purpose in doing what she loved.

"I can't, Deb. I've a new job waiting and a place to stay. Besides, Marta will be great. She loves children, has excellent experience, and is more than ready to get back to work."

"You don't have to sell me on her, I know she'll do fine. I still hate losing you." Tears filled Deb's eyes as she drew her friend into a hug. "Don't forget to send me your address as soon as you arrive. And call me on your trip south." She tried for a smile, failing horribly.

"You'll be the first call I make." She drew back from her friend and yanked her bag of supplies over her shoulder. "Plan to come for a visit when you can make time."

"You can count on it." Deb walked outside, shading her eyes from the early morning sun, and watched Lainey climb into her new, shiny red SUV. At least she'd gotten rid of that piece of junk coupe. "Be safe!" Deb waved as the car faded into the distance.

******

Lainey had one more stop to make before leaving Bluebird Falls. Mark knew of her decision, had tried to talk her out of it, and failed. They'd been good friends for years, and now she had to say goodbye. At least she had a possible temptation to dangle in front of him.

"Mark around?" Lainey walked into the large stone building in the old downtown area. This section of town had been restored block by block over the last few years, reinventing itself in the process, and drawing new businesses to the area. Mark's job as a CPA kept him busy in the booming economy. Even as the rest of the country still languished in recession, Bluebird Falls had been able to thrive.

"Sure is, Lainey. I'll let him know you're here." The receptionist, an older lady with grown children, and a husband who enjoyed fishing, had been with the firm for years. She'd once told Lainey she planned to die on the job. None of this retirement nonsense for her.

"Hey." Mark walked up and gave her a quick peck on the cheek. "So this is it, huh?"

33

Lainey nodded, afraid she'd lose it if she spoke. Mark saw her eyes mist over and grabbed her elbow.

"Come on. I'll get you some coffee for the road."

Their favorite coffee place was a block away. They made the best lattes for miles around and it had become a ritual for them to meet once a week at the little shop to catch up.

"Hi, Mark. Two lattes coming up," the teenage barista called as they entered.

"Make one a large," Mark called back. "And one of those croissant things she likes." He looked at Lainey. "For the road."

"How's work going?" Lainey asked as she settled into her seat.

"Normal stuff. Pretty routine right now." He thanked the young man who brought their drinks and took a sip of his latte. "How far you going today?"

"Some place near St. Gregg. It's about halfway and I hear they have lots of motels." She held the cup up to sip the hot brew, then smiled, satisfied at how good it tasted.

"You're sure about this? I can't change your mind?"

"It's something I have to do. Besides, the opportunity is just too good to pass up. The chance to own a preschool plus an option on her house, which is where I'll live—at least until I decide to purchase or buy another place."

"You said she's retiring?"

"And leaving the area. All her kids are in this area of Idaho. That's how I found out about it, through her daughter whose son is a student at Deb's school. I'll work with her for a couple of months, learn the system, and get to know the kids and parents, then make a decision." She sipped at her latte, then sat back in her chair. "I have the money from my parents' estate and I've dreamed of this for years. Somehow it just feels right."

"And if it's not what you want?"

"Hey, preschools are always looking for teachers. I'll find something."

Mark watched Lainey's eyes sparkle as she spoke, and as often happened, he got swept into the excitement with her. He'd miss her but was also glad for her. "Who's looking at the books for you?"

"Well, I hoped you might offer." She hadn't wanted to take advantage of their friendship by asking for his input on the financials before. Lainey had looked them over with Deb. Both thought everything seemed in order, yet she really wanted a professional's opinion.

"Of course. Do you have them with you?"

"A copy is in the car."

"Perfect. I'll check them out and have my questions ready by the time you arrive in Arizona."

"That would be wonderful." She finished her coffee and set the cup down. "I do have something else to discuss with you."

"Fire away."

"There's a small CPA firm looking for a third partner. According to Helen, the woman who is selling the preschool, the two partners, both women, prefer to find a male to buy in."

"And why would I want to leave what I have and start over someplace where it's hot, and dry, with no trees?" He shook his head. "No. I'm fine here. Besides, maybe you'll hate it and move back north."

"That's doubtful if the deal works out. I've done a lot of research and where I'm going is in a mountain area, with trees, lakes, hiking, and some snow in the wintertime. And it's growing. Something to consider."

"I'm always open to opportunity—just warning you that this town suits me fine."

"Fair enough. But don't think I won't send you anything I learn about the firm. You never know." Lainey smiled, hoping she could lure him down for a visit.

******

"What can I get you, Missy?" The older, bearded man stood at the counter of a small motel in southern Utah. It appeared clean, not far from the freeway, and next door to a coffee shop that served twenty-four hours a day.

"One room. Non-smoking, please." Lainey fished in her purse for her wallet.

"One key or two?"

"One. How's the place next door?"

"Basic food. Clean, reasonable."

That sounded perfect.

"If you want a good breakfast, Ethel's south on the freeway is the best choice."

"Appreciate the tip."

"You need help with anything, give me a call."

"Thanks."

She checked her phone which started to ring as she walked to the restaurant. Robert. He'd called several times today, leaving messages when she didn't answer. She hoped he'd take the hint and realize they were over.

Lainey grabbed a quick dinner then settled into her room, leaning against the headboard with a book she'd put off reading for months—an historical western romance, set in the ranchlands of northern Arizona. It was an interesting story, with a strong, handsome male character. He had blond hair and warm brown eyes, and in her mind, he was the exact image of Cameron Sinclair.

She closed her eyes and remembered how he'd been with the lost Scouts. They'd each hugged him before leaving with their parents. His smile had been gentle, kind, even though he'd been bone tired from the search.

Lainey hadn't reached out to him. She had his email and knew he lived somewhere in Arizona, but that was all. Maybe someday, once she'd settled into her new home, she'd email him, see if he still had an interest in connecting. Lainey doubted it. Long-distance friendships were hard to keep up. Besides, someone like him would be fighting women off, not needing to seek one out.

She fell asleep with the image of a tall, lean, handsome rescue worker fixed in her head.

Chapter Four

"What do you think?" Lainey sat at the small table in her month-to-month rental with financials spread out, her phone clamped between her shoulder and ear, speaking with Mark, who'd received the most recent documents a couple of days before.

"I can't find anything wrong." Mark flipped through his notes as he held the phone to his ear with his other hand. "She's had the business for twenty years, the profits are consistent, and like you said, there's room to expand, add a private kindergarten or additional preschool space. That's the only way you'll be able to increase your income."

"And the sales price?"

"I think there may be room for negotiation. She's including her house in the total amount. That's the part I believe to be a little high, especially given the real estate market in your area." Mark paused a moment. "My question is, do you like the house?"

"I love it and she's kept it up. It's in a good location, a few blocks from the old downtown, and a mile from the preschool. Still, I don't want to over pay."

"Tell you what. I'm due for a break. How about I come down, see the house and business in person, and give you my opinion?"

Relief washed over Lainey. "That would be wonderful."

"Good. Today's Wednesday. How about I come down next Friday and plan to stay through Tuesday? That should give us plenty of time."

"Whatever works with your schedule. I really appreciate it."

They hung up with Lainey feeling optimistic about the business and the house. If the purchase went through, she'd be buying a nice Victorian with restored kitchen and baths. It came with some furniture, so she wouldn't need to put much money into it right away.

She walked toward the small convenience kitchen in her rented apartment and pulled down a cup for tea. The edge of a small piece of paper hiding beneath a magazine on the counter caught her attention. Lainey pulled it out—Cameron's email. She stared at it, then stuffed it into her pocket.

An hour later she finished the last of her work and pushed back from the computer, then thought of the piece of paper in her pocket. Why not? She typed out a quick email message to Cameron. The odds he'd respond after all this time were slim. She pressed Send, then headed to bed, never expecting to hear back, yet hopeful she would.

******

Cam stretched out his long legs and lifted his hands behind his head before leaning back into the large, tapestry covered sofa in Megan's living room. They'd been seeing each other for several weeks—dinners, movies, lunch a few times, riding horses around the ranch, and even driving to Phoenix for a hockey game.

He enjoyed her company. No drama, no stress, and easy conversation. They had a slow, steady pace with no surprises or commitments—and no sparks. That seemed to be the part holding Cam back from letting himself get any closer. He was attracted to Megan, and even though they'd slept together a couple of times, he still felt no overwhelming pull, no electricity, or desire to reach out and draw her to him. Their relationship was consistent and predictable—exactly what he wanted. It worked, and with his hectic schedule, it seemed the best type of situation. He could walk away at any time if he felt pressure from Megan, even though he sensed she felt the same way he did. At this point, he had no desire for anything more.

"Here you go. One coffee." Megan handed Cam the cup and sat down next to him. "Do you want to watch a movie?"

He sat up, cradling the hot cup. "If you don't mind, I think I'll head home. I have a big day tomorrow with the board meeting. How about we go out Friday night?"

"That's fine. I'm pretty bushed also."

Cam drove the half-hour to his cabin, thinking of where to take Megan to dinner. He heard the new steak house had a great dessert menu. She loved dessert. He already knew what she'd order. Steak, medium, a baked potato with butter and nothing else, steamed vegetables, no bread, and dessert. She'd eat half the steak, half the potato, and all of the dessert. Nothing like her business partner, Zell, who always cleaned her plate and still had dessert.

He chuckled when he thought of Eric and Zell. They'd been going out as long as Cam and Megan, yet their relationship appeared to be the polar opposite of his. Both were energetic, headstrong, and driven. He'd seen them go head-to-head several times on what Cam considered small issues—the choice of a restaurant or who picked out a movie. Eric and Zell were both competitive, almost to a fault.

Even though Cam liked Zell, he just couldn't see Eric spending his life with a woman who aggravated him much of the time. Cam was surprised the two had lasted this long.

He closed the front door, threw his keys on the dining room table, and walked into the second bedroom where he kept his computer, turning it on while he changed clothes. Cam grabbed a glass of water and sat down to see emails loading. One caught his attention right off. He didn't recognize the address and almost hit Delete before changing his mind and opening it. His gaze froze on the name at the bottom. Lainey Devlin.

Cam scanned the short message. She said nothing about her fiancé or job, or much of anything, really. She asked how things were going with him and mentioned she had some changes coming into her life. *What does that mean?* Cam wondered. The message ended with an invitation to email back if he still had an interest in connecting. An interest? Hell, yes, he still had an interest. Then he thought of Megan and the ease of their situation. He guessed any involvement with Lainey would require work and compete with the life he pursued.

Cam pushed away from the computer, turned off the light, and walked across the hall to his bedroom, an image of Lainey rolling across his mind. Ebony hair, infectious smile, and the most beautiful emerald green eyes he'd ever seen—eyes that drew him in—wide, honest, and searching.

He threw himself onto the bed, covering his eyes with an arm, and tried to understand what it was about her that fascinated him so. Yes, he'd found her attractive, even in her rescue gear with soot and dirt smeared across her face and hands, fierce determination evident in the set of her jaw and mouth. The intensity he saw in her eyes as she dragged the female hiker down the mountain had left no doubt in Cam's mind that Lainey would have saved the woman or died trying. Her mental strength captivated him.

His thoughts drifted to the email and what she didn't say.

Cam sat up and swung his legs around to stand, then stopped. He had to make up his mind how far he'd be willing to go in his pursuit of Lainey if he found out she'd called off her engagement. And that's what it would be—absolute pursuit. Even though she lived in another state, there wasn't a doubt in Cam's mind he'd go after her with a single-mindedness imbedded in his genes. And that pursuit would be at the expense of the goals that had always mattered to him the most.

******

Lainey sat up, drenched in sweat and shaking. It had been a long night, with little sleep, interrupted by strange dreams, including one that jolted her awake. She'd grabbed a glass of water and gulped it down, searching for calm. Her eyes landed on the clock. Two in the morning. She hadn't had the dream for years and thought it had been relegated to her past.

Flames, screams, people rushing past while pointing toward something behind them. Even in her sleep, she could sense her heart rate quicken. Her eyes darted in one direction then another as hot, leaping streams of fire surrounded her. An explosion pierced the air before a massive wall of water appeared overhead, crashing around her, and sweeping everything into some unseen darkness.

Lainey shook her head, forcing her thoughts to the present. Her eyes darted around the bedroom, searching for the television remote that lay a few feet away. She clicked the power button, settled against her headboard, then gave up after fifteen minutes and slipped back under the covers. The old clock that had belonged to her mother continued to jump from minute to minute, marking off the passage of time. Sometime during the early hours she'd drifted off.

Lainey woke to bright light streaming through her bedroom window and the sounds of children playing outside. She jumped out of bed when she saw the time, made coffee and fired up her computer, waiting as emails downloaded. She scanned them in quick fashion, and a tinge of disappointment washed over her when no response from Cameron appeared. It was Saturday. Maybe he'd gone out of town, perhaps on a rescue mission and hadn't seen her message. Regardless, she had work to do.

By noon she'd spoken with Helen, the owner of the preschool. They scheduled a time to walk through the house with Mark, visit the preschool, and meet afterwards.

Checking her email once more, Lainey spotted a message from Mark asking that she provide a contact at the CPA firm looking for an additional partner. He didn't come out and state his interest, although Lainey had trouble keeping her excitement under control at the realization Mark had decided to consider it. She picked up the phone and called Helen, who'd first mentioned the firm. Within minutes she'd sent Mark what he needed.

Lainey looked at her to-do list for the day. She grabbed her purse and dashed out the door.

"Hi. May I help you?"

The man behind the desk looked familiar. Lainey pushed the thought aside as she stepped forward and stuck out her hand.

"I'm Lainey Devlin. It looks like I'll be buying a business in town and want to find out if you have a need for more SAR volunteers."

He clasped her hand. "Frank Moretti. We're always looking. Do you have any experience?"

"Yes, sir. I have a little over four years in SAR and have completed numerous mountain rescues, and a few mounted rescues with my team in Idaho. I'd very much like to get involved here, if there's room."

"Idaho, huh? Were you part of the Montana rescue a few months ago?"

"Yes. And the one at Castle Canyon in Colorado."

"That one turned out real well." He reached into a drawer and pulled out an enrollment packet. "Complete this and bring it back. Or, you're welcome to sit over there, if you have the time."

Lainey took the envelope and smiled. "I'd like to do it now."

"Great. Just call me when you're done. I'll be in the back for a while."

Frank pushed through the doors to the gear and operations area to see Cam walking through the back door, carrying a backpack in one hand and a cup holder with coffees in the other.

"Hey, Cam. What brings you in today?" Frank accepted the coffee and sat on a stool near the lockers.

"Need to drop off my extra pack. It's in pathetic shape after the search a few weeks ago." He looked toward the open back door. "You get a new SUV?"

"SUV?"

"Yeah, a shiny red one parked out front."

"It must belong to the woman in the office. She came in to complete the paperwork for admission to the team. Has some experience. We could use at least one more person."

"Hope she's good."

"According to her she's done some mountain and mounted rescues. I'll check out her application first of the week. You want to meet her?"

"No, don't have time. Eric and Heath are expecting me at the ranch. Mom's planning a BBQ tomorrow and requested all of us be in attendance to setup."

"Well, Cam, a man's gotta do...and all that." Frank pitched the empty cup into a trash can. "Guess I'd better see if she's finished up. I'll invite her to our next meeting if everything checks out."

"See you then, if not before." Cam left the way he came, glancing once more at the SUV and hoping Frank and Jake would find her suitable for the team. In his mind, you could never have too many trained volunteers ready to respond to an emergency.

"You all done?" Frank stepped next to Lainey who handed him the completed forms.

"Here you go. When will I know?"

"In a hurry to get on board?" Frank asked as he looked over the paperwork.

"Always."

"Good. I should be able to get back to you by midweek." He stuck out his hand. "Pleasure to meet you, Lainey."

"Same here." She pulled her car keys out of a pocket and turned to leave.

"By the way, if everything checks out, I'd like you to be at our next meeting. Week after this on Wednesday night."

"I'll block it off now," she smiled back at him and pushed through the door.

Lainey pulled a small piece of paper from her purse. SAR application, post office, grocery store, car wash, gas— her list for the day.

She checked off each in turn, walking through the door to her apartment an hour later and setting the grocery bags on the counter. Four o'clock on a Saturday and her day was done. Now what?

She read through all the material on the preschool until her eyes felt buggy, pulled an energy drink from the refrigerator, and fell onto the sofa. Her eyes roamed the small apartment, searching for something that would hold her attention until she took her evening run. Maybe a stop at the YMCA gym would be good, too.

Her eyes landed on the laptop.

Lainey opened her email and read a confirmation from Mark that he'd received the information and already spoken with one of the partners. He'd be meeting with them during his trip, which he'd extended for a few days. She glanced at the other messages, one from Deb in

Bluebird Falls, asking her to call when she had time, three messages from Robert, who she'd been ignoring since her arrival, and a couple from friends on her former SAR team. No response from Cameron.

She changed clothes, jumped into her car, and headed toward one of the lakes. The day was clear and warm, drawing a lot of families to the popular picnic and campground areas. Stowing her purse under the seat, she stuffed her keys in a pocket, pulled her hair into a ponytail, and started at a slow jog down the trail to the lake.

******

Cam parked as his phone began to ring. He glanced at the caller ID.

"Hi Eric, what's up?"

"You took off before mom could find you. She wants you to bring Megan to the BBQ tomorrow."

"Sure, if she's available. Last night at dinner she mentioned something about being in Phoenix today and tomorrow. I'll check. Are you bringing Zell?"

"I don't know. We got into another one of our disagreements last night. She stormed out and I haven't spoken to her since. Something stupid."

"Like all of them."

"Guess so. The making up is good, just don't know if the angst in between is worth it. What can I say?"

Even the flip response couldn't hide Eric's frustration with the woman he'd been dating.

"Why don't you call it quits and move on?" Cam had asked this same question a couple of weeks before and watched Eric balk.

"Hell, I don't know."

Cameron paused a minute. "You ever hear from Amber?"

Eric's silence told Cam all he needed to know. Eric's high school and college sweetheart, the woman everyone thought he'd marry, had abruptly changed direction during their junior year in college. A drama major, she'd met a professor who encouraged her to move to New York to pursue her dream of acting on the stage. She'd begged Eric to move east with her, transfer to one of the schools in New York, and finish his degree. He'd been too stunned and angry at the time to think it all through. Instead of giving it time, looking at the possibility of supporting her dream, Eric had told her to make a decision—him or New York.

She'd given him two weeks to reconsider. When he held firm, she made her choice. New York.

"Well, you sure did go from one extreme to the other. Amber to Zell. Who would've thought?"

"Yeah, who would've thought?" Eric's voice had lost all hint of life, making Cam wish he'd never brought up Amber's name.

"I'll call Megan, then let mom know. Regardless, I'll see you tomorrow."

Cam closed the phone and slid it in his pocket as his eyes locked on a runner on the other side of the lake.

Something about her seemed familiar, he just couldn't pinpoint what. The woman was in shorts and a t-shirt, her dark hair pulled into a ponytail that swayed as she ran along the trail. He pulled his eyes away and once more, an image of Lainey flashed through his mind.

As much as his mind told him he had no business getting into anything more complicated than what he had with Megan, he still yearned to see Lainey one more time, spend a day with her. The chance lay back at his house, waiting in the email file on his computer. All he had to do was respond, ask some questions, and hit Send.

Chapter Five

"About time you showed up." Eric walked over with a can of beer in each hand, and gave one to Cam.

"Thought we said noon." Cam swallowed the cold liquid and looked up to survey the scene. "How many is Mom expecting anyway?"

"About a hundred people."

"A hundred?" Cam's eyes widened. "I thought she invited family and few friends."

"She did, plus the ranch hands and their families. At least the ones that live on the property. Cassie is coming up from Phoenix, Matt Garner will meet her here along with the rest of the Garner clan. The list just keeps going. We thought Trey, Jesse, and Trevor would be here but they had to cancel at the last minute."

"Where's Zell?"

"I didn't invite her. It's time for us to take a break—maybe a long one. Megan?"

"She's in Phoenix and not coming back for a few days. She did mention they have a lead on a potential partner to buy into their firm. Some guy from out of state. He'll be here the end of the week."

"Zell never mentioned it to me. Guess that tells you the state of our relationship." Eric finished his beer and pitched the empty can into the recycle basket.

"Has anyone heard from Brooke?"

Eric shook his head, disgust evident in the set of his eyes and mouth. "She bailed, like always. I don't know what's going on with her. Ever since that dic..., uh, jerk, Perry, dumped her for his married college professor, she's been a wreck. I'm thinking we need to make a trip out there and find out what's going on."

Cam thought of his younger sister. She'd always been the girl-next-door type, smart, pretty in a cute way, and way too trusting. Neither he nor Eric had liked Perry, an egotistical PhD candidate who thought way too much of himself and too little of Brooke.

"Hey, you two. How about some help over here?" Their stepfather, Heath MacLaren, waved as he pulled a couple of coolers out of a shed several yards way.

"We're on it, Heath," Eric called as the brothers took off at a jog toward the shed. "About Brooke, I do think someone should head out there to check things out."

"We'd better talk with Mom, get her thoughts."

"Talk to me about what?" Annie asked as she walked up and gave Cam a hug.

"Brooke." Eric pulled the shed door open, grabbed one cooler and handed it to Cam, then pulled out one more. "What's going on with her?"

"I wish I knew." Annie shaded her eyes and looked toward the large, outdoor patio where most of the guests would congregate. "She called this morning, apologized for missing her flight and said she'd make it out another time." Annie dropped her arm to her side. "It's not like her to miss flights, or..."

"Blow off family," Cam finished for his mother.

"We think someone should go out there, find out what's going on. She's slipping away and we don't know why." Eric and Brooke had been close growing up, and that relationship had continued, at least until Perry's secret affair had become known. Brooke had clammed up, retreated within herself, making time for her studies but little else.

"No one has seen her since Trey and Jesse's wedding." Cam dropped the cooler next to the ones outside the back door and turned toward his mother.

"And she seemed distressed the entire time. At first I thought her studies had worn her down. Now, well, I think Brooke hadn't gotten over Perry leaving her, or his betrayal of having an affair with her senior advisor—a married woman for crying out loud." Annie found it hard to contain her loathing of Brooke's former fiancé. "I should have taken the time to pull her aside, find out what was bothering her."

"Don't blame yourself, Mom. You were helping Jesse with the wedding, plus planning the reception. All of us could see something was bothering her and no one took the time to push Brooke on it."

"I'll talk with Heath and arrange a time to visit her." Annie heard a car pull up and turned to wave at her brother-in-law, Jace MacLaren, and his wife, Annie's good friend, Caroline. "Looks like the party's starting."

******

"Lainey?"

She recognized the New York accent. "Hello, Frank."

"Guess the accent gave me away."

"Does that happen often?" Lainey joked.

"All the time. Anyway, I spoke with your group in Idaho and they couldn't say enough good things about you. You've had quite a number of missions in four years."

"I'm not sure if that's good or bad, but yes, I've been involved in a lot of call outs."

"I've spoken to our team leader and he's all for asking you to join us. Congratulations."

Relief washed over her. "That's great news. Thanks so much."

"Be at the SAR headquarters next Wednesday at six o'clock. I'll look forward to introducing you to your new team."

"I'll be there." Lainey hung up and sat on a nearby chair. She hadn't realized until that moment how much she'd counted on getting accepted into the local group. She wanted to celebrate, have a drink and toast herself. Unfortunately, she had no one to celebrate with her. Besides, noon on a Wednesday wasn't the time to pour herself a congratulatory cocktail. Instead, she opted for the gym and another run.

Thirty minutes later, she'd parked her car and started off down the deserted trail. It was a windy day with dark clouds moving in from the southwest and the feel of rain in the air. Even the exertion of running didn't stop the increasingly cold wind from chilling her skin. She pulled her lightweight jacket from around her waist and slipped in on. It had been about thirty minutes—a good time to turn around and head back.

She stopped at what sounded like crying coming from behind her and up a small hill. Lainey had heard about a mountain lion that wandered the area from a park ranger the previous week. He'd warned her to be cautious.

"Hello! Is someone up there?" She pulled off her sunglasses and scanned the area, seeing nothing. Deciding the wind had caused the noise, she started toward her car. She hadn't taken four steps when the sound came again, more insistent and urgent this time. Not a mountain lion.

"Hey! Who's up there?" Lainey started up the hillside, slipping on the damp ground and loose leaves a couple of times before stopping halfway to the top. "Anyone around here?"

That's when the crying started in earnest.

Lainey twisted from side to side, trying to locate the sound. "Where are you?" she called once, then twice, before she saw it. A small cave several yards away. She dashed to the opening and peered inside. It wasn't deep, perhaps six feet deep, three feet wide and five feet high. Thank God it wasn't night or she'd have missed the small form huddled at the back.

"You're okay, honey. I'm here." Lainey continued forward at a slow pace, crouching low and whispering to the frightened child. "Are you lost?"

The little girl stared, wide-eyed, her body shaking from what Lainey believed to be both cold and fear.

"I won't hurt you, sweetheart. Can you tell me your name?" The girl hunkered a little further back, still shaking.

Lainey moved onto her knees in front of the girl and touched her hair. "Are you hurt, honey?" She reached into a pocket and pulled out a crunched, yet still edible, granola bar, tore it open, and held it out.

"Mia."

Lainey almost missed the soft whisper.

"Mia? Is that your name?"

She shook her head and took a bite of the bar Lainey had provided.

"Are you hurt?"

"No. I'm cold."

Lainey carefully ran her hands over Mia's body, finding nothing except a few scrapes and bruising.

"Did you lose your parents?"

Mia shook her head. "I ran away."

That took Lainey by surprise.

"How old are you, Mia?"

"Five." Lainey had guessed as much.

"Okay. Let's get you out of here and into something warm. Then we'll talk and you can tell me why you ran away. Sound all right?"

She guided the little girl out of the cave, down the hill, and toward her car, watching for any sign of an adult who might be looking for Mia. She saw no one.

Lainey always carried an extra blanket, socks, and dry shoes in her car. Right now, all she needed was the blanket. It wrapped around Mia twice, calming her trembling, as Lainey asked questions, coaxing her to say more about her parents.

"What's your last name, Mia?"

"Stanton," Mia mumbled before her eyes shot back to Lainey. "I can to go my Grandma's. She will let me stay with her."

"Who is your Grandma?"

"My Grandma Kearney."

"Do you know her first name?"

Mia shook her head.

"Can you show me where she lives?"

"I don't how to get there." Tears began to well in Mia's eyes and Lainey put an arm around her.

Lainey's mind raced. "Tell you what. Would you like to meet some nice people who might know how to help you?"

"I just want to see my Grandma."

"I know, honey. I think my friends can help. Let's get you into a seat belt and see what we can do."

It didn't take Lainey long to get to SAR headquarters. Although her first thought had been the county offices or police, she eliminated those choices, knowing Mia might be placed in some form of child protection program if her parents couldn't be found right away. She'd check with the people at SAR, most of whom had lived in the area a while. If no one knew the family, Lainey would have no choice but to take her to the county.

Lainey walked around the car and held her arms out to Mia. "Come on, kiddo, let's go inside and get you some hot chocolate."

"Well, hello, Lainey. Didn't expect to see you until next Wednesday." Frank Moretti stood near the wall where he'd been posting updated information on past searches. "And who do you have with you?"

"This is Mia." She looked down at the little girl who stood ramrod straight against Lainey's leg. "Mia, this is Mr. Moretti."

Frank sauntered over and knelt in front of the girl. "Hello, Mia. Glad to meet you. She a relative?"

"No. I was on a run at Golden Lake and found her hiding in a cave." She glanced down at Mia. "Come on, honey, let's get that hot chocolate I promised you." Lainey glanced at Frank. "You do have hot chocolate, right?"

He looked offended, then smiled. "Of course we do. What kind of a rescue center would this be without hot cocoa? Come on."

While Mia sat drinking the warm liquid, Lainey and Frank stood in the corner, talking in low tones.

"She says she ran away from home. I believe her last name is Stanton. She used to live with her grandma but now lives with her father. She's five and says her grandma's last name is Kearney."

"And you found her off the county road at the lake?"

"Yes, in a cave at the south end."

Frank scratched his chin. "I can't think of anyone I know with the last name of Stanton who lives out that way. Darrel Stanton and his wife live on the other side of town, but their kids are older."

Both turned at the sound of the back door opening.

"Frank," the man nodded.

"Jake. This is Lainey Devlin, the new volunteer."

He held out his hand. "Nice to meet you, Lainey. I'm Jake Renner, the team lead." He glanced over at the little girl. "She yours?"

Frank jumped in before Lainey could respond. "She found little Mia hiding out by Golden Lake. Told Lainey she's running away."

"Mia?" Jake asked, his expression changing from curiosity to disbelief. He walked closer to the child, then sat down. "Hey, Mia. Do you remember me?"

"Uh huh. You're Mister Jake."

"That's right. Do you want to tell me what's going on? Where's your Grandma?"

"I don't know."

"What happened?" Jake looked over his shoulder at Frank and Lainey, confusion showing on his face.

"My daddy took me away today."

Jake scrubbed a hand down his face and shook his head. "Okay, honey. We'll sort this out real soon. You all right for now?"

Mia concentrated on the last of her cocoa.

Jake pushed from the table and walked toward the others. "I know her grandma. Marge Kearney. Nice lady.

59

She's had custody of Mia since she was maybe one or two. Her mother died while her father was in prison. He must've been released. I can't think of a reason why Marge would let Mia go. She has no use for her ex-son-in-law."

"What now?" Lainey pulled her jacket more fully around her as a slight breeze came through the open door.

"If she'll let me, I'll take her by Marge's house, and find out what's going on."

"What did her father do?" Frank looked around Jake to check on Mia.

"Drug bust of some type. One of many from what I understand."

"Is it all right if I go with you?" Lainey didn't want to leave Mia alone, even though the girl knew Jake.

"Sure. Let me drop off the stuff in my car and we'll get going. You can follow me."

Chapter Six

Lainey dropped her keys on the counter and headed toward the shower, exhausted and pleased. She thought about the events of the last few hours.

She and Jake had gone by Marge Kearney's home and found two patrol cars out front. They'd strolled to the front door, each holding one of Mia's hands, the girl's eyes wide at the sight of several uniformed men in her Grandma's yard.

"Hey. What's going on?"

"Hi, Jake." The officer looked down. "That wouldn't be Mia, would it?"

"Sure is. What happened?"

The officer cast another glance at Mia before looking back at Jake. "Marge Kearney let Mia go to a friend's house this morning to play. The friend's mother called all upset because some man had come by and taken Mia from the front yard. The woman's daughter told her the man said he was Mia's father. All we can figure is he must have followed Mia to the friend's house after she left her Grandma's this morning."

"Mia!"

"Grandma!" Mia dropped Jake and Lainey's hands to run to the older woman who stood at the top of the porch.

Marge saw Jake approach over her granddaughter's shoulder and stood.

"Did you find her, Jake?"

"Marge, this is Lainey Devlin, our newest volunteer. She found Mia while on a run at Golden Lake. Mia told Lainey she had run away."

"Damn that Karl," Marge hissed then clamped a hand over her mouth.

"Sounds like he's out."

"Last week. Wants custody back, but I told him there was no chance I'd let him take Mia away. I've been assured that I'm her legal guardian and that's how it's going to stay."

They'd talked a while longer before Jake and Lainey took off.

Now all Lainey wanted to do was cleanup and relax. Maybe she'd order noodles from the take-out place down the street.

She dried her hair, dressed, then walked by the table in her living room and spotted the computer. Cameron had never returned her email. It stung a little that she'd reached out and he'd ignored her, even if it had taken Lainey weeks to send him a message.

More than anything, it irked her that his lack of response bothered her so much. She'd only met the man twice, and for short periods of time, yet she'd had little success forgetting his earnest, handsome face, or what she'd thought of as an interest in connecting.

Nevertheless, Lainey opened her email, her eyes freezing on one message. Cameron had responded. He said he'd been hung-up with family issues and how glad he'd been to get her email. He asked what she meant by changes in her life and ended with a request for her to stay in touch. Lainey drew in a breath and wondered how much she should share with him, deciding it might be best to keep some things to herself, at least for a while.

She heard her phone ring and grabbed it from inside her purse.

"Lainey?"

"Hi, Mark. You still coming on Friday?"

"Actually, I'll be there tomorrow morning. That okay?"

"Perfect. You all right bunking down on my hide-a-bed or do you want me to get you a room someplace?"

"Your sofa's fine. Any chance you can pick me up at the airport at eleven o'clock?"

"No problem at all. It'll be so good to see you."

"Be there tomorrow." Mark clicked off, leaving Lainey to mentally check off the list of things to do tonight instead of tomorrow. She couldn't wait to see him.

******

Cam dashed through the cabin, grabbing his jacket and hat, then looked around for his car keys. He had a jammed schedule at work, then he planned to take Megan out to dinner.

He looked around the kitchen and into the living room before checking his bedroom once more. That's when he remembered dropping the keys next to his computer the night before. Cam started to pick them up when his eyes caught the screen, still open to his email program. He scrolled down to see a new message from Lainey.

Cam opened and read through it. She mentioned her continued involvement in SAR and that she was considering buying her own preschool. She had a CPA looking over the financials and hoped to have a final decision within a week. Again, no mention of her engagement. He closed his computer, knowing he'd respond, just not right now.

He arrived at the office to receive an added assignment to co-pilot the jet for a meeting Heath had in Denver. Ever since the former company pilot had retired a few months back, Cam had assumed the co-pilot responsibilities. Todd Franks, the man who'd been the co-pilot for years, had been promoted to chief pilot. Cam loved flying the jet. Between his co-piloting position, his job as head of IT, and being the only helicopter pilot for the company, Cam found his days full and rewarding.

Cam and Todd got busy preparing the jet for their flight. He'd rescheduled a couple of meetings and begged off a lunch appointment. Then, at the last minute, the people in Denver cancelled the flight. By then, the entire day had been blown.

He checked his watch as his phone rang.

"Hi, Megan. I'm on my way."

"Come to the office instead. My meeting with the potential partner will finish up in about fifteen minutes. We'll leave from here."

"See you in a few minutes." Cam slid the phone into his pocket. He'd forgotten about her big meeting today.

Cam parked in front of her office as a red SUV pulled away from the curb. He watched as it drove past his truck and noticed a man in the passenger seat and a woman with short, dark hair driving. Cam assumed the man was the potential partner Megan had spoken about. He glanced toward Megan's office in time to see her step out, a jacket over her arm.

She dashed down the steps, got into his car, and placed a quick kiss on Cam's cheek.

Cam pulled away and looked down at her. "The meeting went well?"

"Oh, yeah. I'll tell you everything at dinner."

******

Mark and Lainey sat in silence on the drive to the restaurant Lainey had picked out. She'd promised to take him someplace with oversized portions and down-home food. She delivered on both.

Mark pushed away his plate, having finished his meatloaf with mashed potatoes and gravy. "That was great."

"Anything else for you two?"

"Just coffee for me. Decaf." Lainey sat back, waiting for Mark to make a decision.

"Same here," Mark responded and sat back in his chair.

"Okay, what are your thoughts?"

Mark hadn't mentioned a word about his meeting with Megan and Zell, the partners in the CPA firm. Lainey had sat in silence, absorbing the conversation and trying to get a feel for how Mark would fit in with the two women. She had no doubt he could work with Megan. Her thoughts on Zell weren't so certain.

"It appears to be a solid business, and growing. They're making all the right moves as far as their marketing efforts. The financials look to be in order and they own the building. That's quite an accomplishment in a short period of time."

"What do you think of the partners?"

"I have no doubts about working with Megan. Zell's a question mark for me. Not enough for me to walk away, just something I need to consider."

"Sounds like they're ready to move as soon as you make a decision."

Mark sipped his coffee, his brows furrowing as he continued to think about the opportunity before him. "I'll have a decision by the time I leave town." He set his cup down and looked at Lainey. "By the way, I like your hair. It looks great."

Lainey's hand reached up to touch the shortened locks. "Thanks. I did it on a whim before I picked you up yesterday, but I'm happy with it."

"Yeah. The team back in Bluebird Falls probably wouldn't even recognize you," he joked as they left the restaurant.

******

Lainey sat at her computer, reading the last, short email from Cam. She hadn't responded to his question about her engagement, instead focusing her last message to him on her excitement about the new business and home she'd be buying. Cam had congratulated her and asked again about her fiancé. Lainey tapped out a quick reply about being swamped and she'd get back to him soon.

Mark had given his approval to the purchase of both the preschool and business after meeting with Helen, the owner, and taking a tour of both properties. He'd been impressed with the layout and operation of the preschool as well as the condition of the house.

Lainey and Helen had settled on a price and signed the required documents. The sale would be final within a few weeks. Lainey was anxious to get into her new home and start work at the school. Tons of ideas for improving the facility and bringing in new children had been penciled out. The time had come to make it her own.

"You ready?" Mark walked into the living room, dressed for their morning run.

"When's your meeting?"

"Not until the afternoon. We have lots of time. Come on. I'll buy lunch if you pull ahead, and stay there."

She drove to a wooded trail several miles away. They'd run a different route each day since Mark had been in town. She hadn't been back to Golden Lake. It had lost much of its appeal after finding Mia crouched in the back of the small cave.

Today's run took them through a narrow, winding trail to a lookout. As usual, Mark let her take off in front before shooting ahead. She'd never been able to keep up with Mark and had long ago accepted the fact.

At one point, Lainey took a wrong turn and stopped in a clearing with an open view of the campground below. Her eyes circled the area to see a man, binoculars in hand, looking in her direction. She watched him a moment before he dropped his hands and turned toward a waiting car. He'd been too far away to see his face. Lainey didn't think much of it. Besides, bird watchers were a common sight in the town as well as avid photographers and nature seekers. She let the incident slip from her mind.

Lainey rounded the final turn to see Mark standing with his hands on hips, staring at the blue sky above and valley below, his hair damp from the run.

"Quite a sight."

"Yes, it is." Lainey bent over to take in a deep breath. "What will your family think if you take the offer and move here?" They'd spoken a lot about the town, late into the evening each of the last two nights, debating its pros and cons, and comparing it to Bluebird Falls. He liked that an active SAR team existed and needed more volunteers. He'd already made up his mind to accompany Lainey to the SAR meeting that night. Even if he wasn't a member of the team, he still held active status in Bluebird Falls.

"It's further away from most of my family, although there are some renegades spread out across the southwest. They'll support whatever I decide."

Lainey smiled, as she did most times when Mark made reference to his Lakota heritage. His dark, black-brown hair and caramel-colored skin were testament to his one-quarter Sioux blood. He'd gotten his gray-blue eyes from his mother, and his slim nose from his European grandmother. The fact that some woman hadn't snapped up her handsome friend had always been a source of amazement to Lainey.

"I'm looking forward to meeting the team tonight and seeing if I'll fit in. That would be a deal killer for me, Lainey."

She'd called Frank, asking if it would be all right to bring a potential volunteer to the meeting that night. Frank had responded right away that he'd welcome the chance to meet another volunteer. "I understand, although I believe you're going to fit right in."

Chapter Seven

Lainey checked herself once more in the mirror, deciding she'd made the right decision to cut her hair. Four inches had been taken off, and the ends now hovered at the base of her jaw, framing her face, and, as the stylist said, showing off her wide-set green eyes. She grabbed her coat before joining Mark in the living room.

"All set." She snatched her keys and headed for the door.

"Hold on a minute." Mark picked up his Bluebird Falls SAR cap and settled it on his head. "Now I'm ready."

She parked several cars away from the back door. An assortment of cars, trucks, and SUVs filled the lot, indicating a good number of people were already inside.

They grabbed cups of coffee and met a few other volunteers before Jake Renner called the meeting to order.

"We're still missing a few people, but we're going to start anyway. I've asked Frank to come up and tell you about some new equipment before I go into the updated training schedule. Frank?"

Mark and Lainey sat back and listened. The format matched the one in the Bluebird Falls SAR team with a few minor fluctuations. The updated training routine sounded good, although Lainey groaned a little at the slight increase in pack weight for their runs.

"Now, let's have some introductions. First..." Jake stopped as the back door opened and closed. "Glad you could finally join us," he called toward the back.

"Same here," the volunteer called back.

Lainey sat up a little straighter and turned her head at the sound of the man's voice—deep, clear, and familiar.

"As I was saying, we have a new volunteer, and another potential volunteer who's in town on business. Our new volunteer has already made an impact by locating a child who'd been reported missing. She can tell you all about it after the meeting. Lainey Devlin, from Bluebird Falls, Idaho. Stand up, Lainey."

Cam's coffee cup stopped halfway to his mouth and his eyes grew wide at the sight of the woman he'd fantasized about for months. She stood, a broad smile radiating from her face as she acknowledged the greetings from those around her. She started to lower herself back into her chair when her eyes caught sight of a lone figure standing by the refreshment table and her knees locked—Cam. Her mouth dropped open and even though she knew curious eyes were focused on her, she couldn't seem to rise or sit. Finally, she sat down, her hands gripping the sides of the chair.

"Welcome Lainey. Now I'd like to introduce you to Mark Hill. He's currently with the Bluebird Falls SAR group in Idaho. He may be buying into a business in Fire Mountain, and if so, we can expect to see him join our ranks. Right, Mark?"

Mark stood and acknowledged the others. "That's right. Hope to have a decision within a few days."

The meeting went on for another few minutes before Jake adjourned for the night, reminding them of the next meeting.

Lainey walked toward the back, introducing herself to a few more volunteers while keeping her gaze searching the area where Cam had been standing. The sight of him, in this room, perhaps twenty feet away, had caused her to feel half full of anticipation while the other half was consumed with dread. He'd looked the same—tall, lean, and strong, and every bit as handsome as she remembered.

She reached the far wall and turned back toward the front of the room, trying to locate him.

"Hello, Lainey."

Startled, she spun around to see Cam standing a foot away, arms folded, radiating cool poise as he locked eyes with hers. Lainey took a step back and took in the sight of him. She'd never seen Cam in anything except his rescue gear. Now he stood before her wearing a dark t-shirt stretched taut across a solid chest and well-defined arms. His broad shoulders tapered into a slim waist and his jeans molded perfectly around his muscled thighs.

"Lainey?"

She looked up to see a knowing grin and amused eyes. Her face heated, knowing he'd caught her staring.

"Hello, Cam."

"You look good, Lainey. I like your hair." He continued to let his eyes wander over her. "Did you come with Mark?"

She raised a hand to the shortened hair while looking behind her to see Mark chatting with a couple of men. "Yes. He's visiting—looking at a potential business opportunity."

Cam's eyes shifted to Mark then back to Lainey. "Have coffee with me. He can find his way home, right?"

Her heart began to thump, an odd, rapid staccato that took her by surprise.

"Yes, I think he can manage." She walked up to Mark and handed him the keys. He grasped them, then looked to the back and nodded at Cam.

"So you've already hooked up with Sinclair."

"It's just coffee."

"Right. Well, don't be out too late," he chided as she strode away.

Lainey climbed into Cam's gun-metal grey pickup and found herself staring again as he slipped behind the wheel. She took a deep breath, steadying her nerves, and trying to restore some confidence. Her body's response to this man was out of control and beyond anything she'd ever experienced.

"This your new town? One of the big changes you mentioned in your email?" Cam focused his gaze ahead, not risking eye contact. He'd been stunned to hear her name and see her stand up, wearing a red fitted top over skintight jeans. His body had responded without hesitancy, the attraction stronger than anything he'd ever felt before.

"Yes, it is." She licked her lips, deciding the time had come to share all her news.

He made a turn and parked on the side of the road next to a family-style restaurant. "It's not fancy but they make great coffee and decadent cinnamon rolls."

They settled into a booth, ordered coffee and rolls, then Cam rested his arms on the table. "So tell me all your news."

"It looks like I'm buying a preschool here in Fire Mountain." Her eyes lit up as she spoke and Cam couldn't help being drawn into her enthusiastic voice. "It's been in town a long time, and the current owner is great. There's a full roster of children, and a house, near the old downtown area, is included in the price. It's perfect."

She stopped as the waitress delivered their order.

Lainey grabbed some sweetener and cream. "I'm very excited about it." She cut a piece of the sticky roll and slid it into her mouth. "Wow, this is wonderful."

"The business and home sound great." He took a sip of the hot coffee. "And your fiancé?"

Lainey set down her fork and took a slow breath. "It's over. I ended it several weeks ago, just before I came here to check out the business. I should have broken it off a long time ago."

Cam kept his pleasure at the news to himself. He had some quick thinking to do about his situation with Megan and the opportunity he had with Lainey. One offered a steady, consistent relationship without demands or expectations—just what Cam needed at this stage of his career.

The other offered excitement, surprises, and, he guessed, much more commitment and a loss of focus on what had always mattered—exactly what he didn't need. His mind reeled at the possibilities. If Lainey's response to him indicated anything, he'd lay odds he had a good chance with her.

"Why didn't you break it off with him sooner?"

Lainey sipped the last of her coffee, reflecting on her engagement and the relief she still felt at calling it off. "I had a packed schedule with work, SAR, plus some involvement in a couple of local children's programs. He hadn't pressured me to give up my job or other activities until the last few months. I guess I thought he'd get over badgering me. One day I realized I just didn't love him and could never mold myself into the wife he wanted. Now I have a fresh start and an open future."

"And Mark?"

"Mark?" She thought a moment. "Oh. No, he and I are friends. Good friends but nothing more. We met in college, found jobs, and moved to Bluebird Falls about the same time." She grinned. "It's funny. I don't think either of us has ever thought of the other as more than a sister or brother. So tell me what's going on with you."

Cam talked about his IT job, as well as flying the company helicopter and co-piloting the jet. Lainey could see the pride in his eyes and hear the enthusiasm in his voice as he spoke of the many projects his stepfather kept giving him.

"It's what I'd always worked toward—working in a complex company where I can make an impact."

"Do you think you'll stay here in Fire Mountain?"

"I'd like to. Much of what I do depends on how my job changes and if I'm offered new opportunities. If I were to select one place to live, it would be here."

"What about your family? Do you have brothers, sisters?"

Cam's eyes sparkled as he told of his blended family. It took a few minutes for him to describe the intricacies of the MacLaren-Sinclair clan and how everyone fit together.

"Your family parties must be entertaining." Lainey loved the idea of a big family and lots of space.

"That they are." Cam checked his watch. "Guess I better get you home." He stood and escorted Lainey to his truck. They spoke little on the way to her apartment.

"This is it." She pointed to a small complex on a side street off the main road.

Cam pulled to a stop and hopped out, walking around to Lainey's side and opening the door. She'd turned to slide down from the truck when Cam lifted her from the seat and slowly set her in front of him.

"I'll walk you to the door."

There were a couple of lights coming from inside and one porch light cast a soft glow over the entry. They stopped as Lainey dug out her keys then glanced at him.

"Thanks for the coffee and roll, and the conversation."

Cam didn't respond, just stared down into her face, his eyes never wavering from hers as he lowered his head to brush his lips lightly against hers, once, then twice. He lifted his face a fraction before capturing her mouth once more, wrapping his arms around her, and pulling her close. He'd fantasized about this for months, yet his dreams didn't come close to what he felt now.

Lainey moved into Cam, wrapped her arms around his neck and pulled him down as his tongue traced the outline of her lips, encouraging her to open for him. He tasted of coffee and cinnamon. She felt his hands roam over her back, down to her hips, then back up. One hand settled at the back of her head, his fingers easing through her hair and holding her in place.

Cam wanted her with an intensity that surprised him. He'd been with many women, been close to commitment at one point, yet none of them affected him like Lainey. The feel of her body aligned with his, her taste, the scent of vanilla and spice that wafted over him whenever she was around, overwhelmed him. He wanted more of Lainey, much more.

Cam pulled back and rested his forehead against hers, his breathing labored, his heart pounding in his chest.

"I knew it would be like this with you," he breathed as he placed one more kiss on her swollen lips.

"It was better than I imagined." Lainey's soft smile and glazed eyes confirmed that she'd been as affected by their kiss as Cam.

He reached into his pocket and pulled out his phone. "Can I have your number now?" he joked.

"I think that's an excellent idea." She gave him her number and he entered it into his phone.

"I'd better go." He kissed her once more then turned to leave. "I'll call you—soon."

Lainey let out a breath and watched him climb into his truck, excitement, desire, and hope washing over her as he pulled away.

******

Cam drove back to his cabin, knowing the time had come for him to have an honest talk with Megan, and break it off.

He pushed open his front door as the phone in his pocket began to vibrate. Cam recognized the number.

"Hi, Megan. What's up?"

"How'd your meeting go?"

Cam hesitated a moment. "Good."

"The man who's interested in the partnership asked if we could go out to dinner with him on Friday. I told him I already had a date, but he said to bring you along. I'd love to get your opinion of him, if you're interested."

"Sure, I can do that. Tell me when to pick you up and where he wants to meet. I assume Zell is coming."

"She is. Thanks, Cam." She paused a moment. "Well, I'll see you Friday about six."

"See you then." He hung up, deciding he'd have his talk with Megan after the dinner on Friday.

Chapter Eight

"You have plans tonight?" Eric strolled into Cam's office at three o'clock on Friday afternoon.

"I'm having dinner with Megan, Zell, and their potential new partner." He looked up from his paperwork and smiled. "You want to come?"

"Hell, no. I haven't spoken with Zell since I called it off, and I hope not to run into her for a while. Nice lady, lots of fun, but pure poison for my peace of mind."

Cam chuckled. "Guess you'll be on the lookout for someone else now that you and Zell are history." He looked back at the papers in front of him.

"Don't know, I kind of like flying solo." Eric started for the door then turned. "Except I did hear about a new SAR volunteer in town. Single, pretty, great body..."

Cam's head jerked up. "She's off limits," he growled, surprised at the edge to his voice.

Eric looked at his brother a moment. He'd never heard Cam respond like this to a comment about an available woman. In fact, Cam rarely snapped at him about anything. Eric lowered himself into a chair. "You want to tell me about it?"

"No." Cam's jaw worked but he said nothing more.

"Okay. You won't talk about it, yet you're ordering me to stay away from her?"

"She's not your type." Cam's eyebrows drew together in a frown.

"And you know because ..."

Cam put his pen down and sat back. "I've met her, more than once on searches and again at the monthly SAR meeting." He ran a hand through his hair as his gaze settled back on Eric. "You can go after any woman you want. I'd never try to stop you."

Eric noted Cam's set expression and fixed eyes. There'd be no messing around on this one.

"I know you wouldn't stop me, and you know I won't go after any woman you have an interest in. The question is, what does she mean to you?"

Cam rose from his chair. "Hell, Eric. I wish I knew." He crossed his arms, settling his hips against the edge of his desk. "I've decided to call it off with Megan. It won't ever go any further for me. As for Lainey, well, I just don't know. She's intelligent, interesting, and everything I'd want if I were looking to settle down and build a family. I'm just not certain my life is ready for a relationship that requires work or time."

"Have you dated her?"

"No."

"But you want to?"

"I'd like to do a lot more than date her, and that's my problem." Cam's mouth tightened. He checked his watch. "I have a meeting downstairs in ten minutes, after that I'm heading home to get ready for dinner."

Eric stood and opened the office door. "Beers tomorrow after the game. No excuses."

Cam let out a breath, irritated at the exchange and angry at himself for responding like such a possessive jerk. He had no claim on Lainey—didn't know for certain if he wanted one. Their kiss had affected him much more than he'd intended. He'd wanted a taste, just enough to see if they had any chemistry. Now he knew a relationship between them wouldn't be anything like his affairs in the past. He'd never had an actual date with her, barely knew her, and already she messed with his mind.

He grabbed the meeting folder and headed downstairs, determined to push her out of his system, at least until he'd broken it off with Megan. If this is how Lainey affected him now, she had the potential to seriously affect everything he'd worked toward. He couldn't afford to get off track, not now, and especially not over his body's reaction to a woman.

******

Eric climbed into his truck and started the engine, letting it idle while he punched in a number on his phone.

"Hey, Brooke, it's Eric. Just checking in to see how you're doing. I hear Mom might be headed your way in a week or so. Call me back."

He set the phone down. His sister still hadn't responded to his emails or messages, and his initial irritation had turned to true worry. He knew their mom was flying out to San Diego within a few days. She'd figure things out.

Eric drove toward The Tavern, a local pub favored by the Friday after-work crowd. He thought of Cam and their discussion a couple of hours earlier. He couldn't recall the last time Cam had sounded so possessive over a woman.

He'd heard about Lainey from one of his friends in the SAR unit, how she'd already found a lost kid, and the way she filled out her tight jeans. Yes, she was already becoming the talk of the singles circuit even if she'd done nothing to warrant the attention. And now to realize Cam had a thing for her shocked Eric. No matter how Cam positioned it, she'd already gotten to him, and damn if Eric wasn't glad.

He pulled into the tavern and got out as Jake Renner parked alongside him.

"Hey, Jake."

"Eric." He looked into the truck. "Cam with you?"

"No. He has dinner plans with Megan tonight."

"Not Lainey Devlin, huh?"

"What do you mean?" Eric opened the tavern door, allowing Jake to walk past.

"They left the SAR meeting together Wednesday night. Went for coffee or something. Anyway, he seemed to be pretty smitten."

"I'll be damned," Eric muttered.

"What'd you say?"

"Nothing. Just surprised. Well, I guess anything's possible."

******

"You sure you don't mind coming along tonight?" Mark sat in the living room, ready for his dinner meeting with Megan and Zell. He'd invited Lainey, believing it would be good for her to get to know the two women better, make some connections in her new home town.

"Not at all. It'll be great to go out for a night. Where are we going?"

"Some steakhouse Megan likes. She mentioned bringing her boyfriend who's some big shot in town. His family is pretty well known in Arizona. My guess is he'd probably be another good connection for each of us."

"Sounds good. I'm always up for meeting new people."

Thirty minutes later Mark opened the door to the Cattle King and followed Lainey inside, noticing the dark wood interior, beautiful oil paintings on the walls, and plush carpet.

"May I help you?"

"We're meeting Megan Morena."

"Please follow me."

Mark spotted Megan and Zell at a round table in the center. He shook their hands and introduced Lainey as they took their seats.

"Your friend coming?" Mark asked Megan.

"He should be here any minute." Megan looked past Lainey to the entrance. "Oh, there he is now." She waved him over.

"Sorry I'm late," Cam leaned down to give Megan a kiss on the cheek, then straightened. His eyes locked on the woman across from Megan, dumbstruck at who sat at their table.

"Cam, this is Mark Hill and Lainey Devlin." She looked up at Cam. "This is Cam Sinclair."

Cam dragged his eyes away from Lainey long enough to shake Mark's hand. "Good to see you again, Mark." He shifted his gaze back to Lainey to see hurt, disappointment, and pain cross her face in a matter of seconds. His stomach clenched as he swallowed the lump in his throat. "Hello, Lainey."

The initial shock Lainey felt had turned to hurt, then anger. Mark's words came back to her. *Megan's bringing her boyfriend. Some big shot in town from a well-known family.* Her gut twisted at her naïve dreams about this man. He'd reached out to her in friendship, acted like he wanted more, and she'd been swept along in her fantasies about the two of them becoming a couple. What a fool she must appear to him after her passionate response to his kisses two nights before. She wanted to bury her face in her hands. Instead, Lainey steeled herself, determined not to let her emotions show.

"Cam. It's good to see you." She forced a smile, hoping the turmoil she felt didn't show.

"You know each other?" Zell asked.

Cam took a seat between Megan and Zell, trying to still the jolt at seeing Megan and Lainey at the same table, while regaining his composure. "Lainey just joined the SAR team. And I believe Mark will be joining us if the deal between you three goes through."

"How wonderful, Mark. It's a great group of people." Megan sipped her wine, oblivious to the tension that sparked across the table.

Lainey focused on her menu, the paintings on the wall, anything except letting her gaze settle on Cam. She could feel his eyes on her, as if they had a direct connection across the table that no one else could sense. Still, she avoided looking at him.

"Lainey?" Mark's words penetrated her thoughts.

"I'm sorry. What?"

"Cam asked if you enjoyed getting to know some of the volunteers."

She took a sip of water, trying to contain her racing heart. "Yes. Everyone seemed professional, committed, and quite welcoming. I believe it will work out fine."

Mark watched Lainey struggle. She spoke little of the night Cam had taken her for coffee, other than to say she thought they might start seeing each other. Mark felt certain she'd developed feelings for Cam Sinclair, more than she wanted to admit, now he knew for certain. If he'd known that Cam and Megan were an item, he never would've asked Lainey to join them. He knew her too well, and the hurt that had crossed her face when Cam walked in and kissed Megan had pained Mark as well.

"What do you do, Lainey?" Zell asked, keeping the conversation going, unaware of the side drama going on around their table.

"I'm a preschool teacher."

"And who do you work for?"

"I'm in the middle of buying the preschool owned by Helen Jorgensen. She's retiring and moving up to Bluebird Falls where her daughter lives."

"Oh, I know the school. From what I hear it's very popular, even has a waiting list." Megan glanced around the table, making up her mind that Mark would fit quite well into their business.

"I'm fortunate to get it."

Cam listened to the exchange, his eyes drifting over Lainey, and felt his insides squeeze tight. He'd made the decision to cut it off with Megan, had planned to do it tonight after dinner. Even though his life allowed little room for a relationship, and he had no plans for anything permanent, he felt compelled to see what could develop with Lainey. No woman had ever gotten under his skin the way she did.

He looked across the table at the woman he'd held in his arms two nights before to see his hopes crumble. When Lainey did glance his way, her eyes were cold and impersonal, lacking all the warmth he'd become accustomed to seeing. Cam felt a sharp ache in his chest as he realized he might never be able to make amends for what she'd seen tonight.

Dinner proceeded at a slow pace, Cam wanting to pull Lainey aside and talk, Lainey wanting to leave and put as much distance between her and Cam Sinclair as possible. The irritation at her reaction to the man burned. She knew little about him, had never anticipated the appearance of a girlfriend, and yet had forged ahead, hoping for something that had little chance of taking root. It seemed so ridiculous when she thought about it.

"Did you enjoy your dinner, Mark?" Megan finished the last of her wine and set the goblet down.

"Best I've had in a long time. Great suggestion for a restaurant. I'll have to come back again."

"Perhaps to celebrate once you've made the decision to be our third partner." Zell had been on her best behavior all night, and everyone, including Mark, seemed to sense it. "When do you think you'll have a decision?"

"I leave on Tuesday. My plan is to give you a decision before then."

"Excellent. Should we schedule a meeting for Monday afternoon?" Zell pressed.

"Let me think through everything once more and call you Monday morning. I'd like a little more time to digest all the information as well as your offer."

"That works," Megan broke in before Zell could push any further. "It's time for me to head home. It's been a long week."

Cam took his cue and rose to pull out Megan's chair. "Good to see you again, Mark. I hope to have you on the SAR team before long."

"You'll be the third person I call once my decision is made." Mark looked toward Lainey. "Ready?"

She didn't answer, just stood, grabbed her jacket, and said quick goodbyes to everyone before heading toward the exit. Mark lingered a moment, discussing a few details with Zell.

"Excuse me a minute, Megan. I want to speak with Lainey." Cam walked at a brisk pace, trying to catch Lainey before she'd gotten too far. "Lainey, wait up."

She heard his voice, ignored it, and continued on, hoping to get inside her car before he followed her any further.

"Lainey, please. Give me a minute."

She slowed her pace, giving up all pretense of not hearing him, and steeling herself for whatever he said, determined to not let him see her disappointment.

Cam stopped next to her. "I should have told you about Megan."

She looked up at him, her heart racing. "Why didn't you? What exactly did you expect from me?"

He shoved a hand through his thick, blond hair. "I don't know what I expected. Friendship, certainly—more than that, maybe."

"And you thought you could have more with me and still keep your girlfriend?"

"No, that's not at all what I thought." He paused a moment, unsure where this conversation was headed or if he should just back off and let her leave. "The truth is, I've never felt such an immediate connection with anyone, ever. There's something about you that draws me, Lainey. I can't get you off my mind."

She could've said the same thing about him a couple of hours ago. A change had rippled through her when Cam walked into the restaurant and up to Megan—as if a door had slammed shut. Whatever fantasies she held for this man had vanished in a heartbeat.

"I'm sorry you feel that way, Cam, because I don't." She looked over his shoulder to see Mark walking toward them. "I'll see you around."

"I'd planned to break it off with Megan tonight." His voice held a quiet emphasis. It wasn't a plea, just a simple statement of fact.

Lainey looked over her shoulder, wishing she were the type of woman who could come up with a flip response. God had blessed her in many ways, with several talents— sarcasm wasn't one of them. She took a shaky breath and turned back toward her car, unable to make her voice work.

Cam's heart broke at the disillusionment he saw in her eyes. He knew she lied about not feeling anything for him—she was as drawn to him as he was to her. Some people wore their emotions for all to see, and Lainey was one of them. He'd lied by omission, not being up front about his current relationship, and now that omission could cost him much more than he'd ever anticipated.

Mark walked up beside him, looked Cam in the eyes, shook his head then left him standing alone in the parking lot. That one gesture told Cam all he needed to know about how Lainey truly felt, yet it did nothing to ease the ache in his chest.

Chapter Nine

Cam hadn't seen Lainey since the dinner three weeks before, and with each passing day he realized how much he'd lost by not being up front with her. To his surprise, the ache he'd felt as she drove away hadn't lessened in time. In fact, it increased a little every day. The next SAR meeting had been scheduled for the following week. He hoped Lainey would attend. At least he could see her even if she had no use for him.

He'd seen little of Megan. Cam had taken her home after the dinner. Their relationship no longer held the appeal it once did, and he'd told her as much. To his immense relief, she'd come to the same conclusion and welcomed the chance to stay friends.

It didn't matter, though, because he'd already ruined his chances with Lainey. He'd move on, focus on his work, and get back to the life he'd been building before Lainey ever set foot in it.

Cam and Megan kept in touch. He'd learned that Mark requested a couple of minor modifications to the agreement before shaking hands with his new partners. In one more week, he'd be in Fire Mountain for good, living in an extra bedroom in Lainey's new home until he could find his own place.

Lainey's deal had closed without a hitch. Cam sent her an email, congratulating her on the purchase and new status as a business owner. She didn't respond.

Cam glanced up from his desk when he heard a tap on his office door and saw Heath MacLaren, his stepfather, walk in with another man behind him. "Good morning, Heath."

"Cam, I'd like you to meet Damon Heitz. He's the founder and chairman of the company we discussed at the last board meeting. Damon, this is my stepson, Cameron Sinclair."

Cam stood to walk around the desk and shake Damon's hand. "It's a pleasure to meet you, Mr. Heitz."

"Good to meet you too, young man."

"I'd like you and Todd to fly Damon back to Cold Creek, Colorado, then have you stay a few days. Tour the facility, see what might fit with our current operations. When you're done, call Todd and he'll make a return trip for you."

Cam's eyes widened with the request. His degree in computer science and a master's in business, plus several years of experience, including a background in acquisitions, had prepared him for this next move. He couldn't have asked for anything better. Heath just offered to let him be the lead on a potential purchase and he found it hard to hide his surprise.

"No problem, Heath." He turned to Damon. "When would you like to leave?"

"Tomorrow morning, first thing."

"We'll be ready for you."

"I'll be back in a few minutes, Cam." Heath escorted Damon outside and returned to Cam's office within minutes. "Thoughts?"

"Truthfully, I'm stunned. Thank you for offering me this opportunity."

"It's what you've wanted, and now you're ready. The financials have been inspected and I've been to the facility several times over the years. Now I need a fresh perspective from someone with experience in acquisitions. I know you did some of that while in San Francisco. Here's the chance to do it for the family."

Cam stared at Heath, unable to speak. His stepfather was right, it's exactly what he'd hoped for and worked toward. They both knew this type of experience had become essential for anyone aspiring to be the president of one of the MacLaren companies. Heath had offered Cam the opportunity to obtain his dream.

"I won't let you down, Heath."

Heath stood and shook Cam's hand. "Hell, son. Don't you think I know that?"

******

Lainey had been busy beyond anything she'd expected. The preschool now had a new owner and new name—Sunshine Preschool. She'd requested names from parents, considered each one, and finally settled on Sunshine. Helen cut the apprenticeship short when her daughter came down with pneumonia. She'd already packed everything she planned to take and left a few days later, apologizing and promising to return if Lainey needed her help.

Her new home had come with almost all the furniture, everything still in excellent condition, including several antiques. Each day, she woke up feeling good about her decision to move and looking forward to what may lie ahead. Except for the continuing dull ache in the middle of her chest, life was perfect.

Mark would be moving into her place the following week and both planned to attend the next SAR meeting. She hoped they'd still be partners. Frank had already told her that Jake would consider her request, but he'd make the final decision on volunteer assignments.

Lainey glanced at her watch. Six o'clock on Friday evening. All the children had gone home, the toys stowed away, and the place cleaned. The one remaining helper had left thirty minutes earlier, eager to meet her date for dinner. A hot bath and glass of wine now topped Lainey's list.

She walked out toward her car, a strange sense of being watched causing the hairs on her neck to bristle. Lainey glanced around the dimly lit lot. The one outside light didn't illuminate the area like it should, and she vowed to have several more installed the following week. She unlocked her door as a strong scent of alcohol wafted over her. Again she glanced around and saw no one, even though her gut told her something didn't seem right. She climbed inside, locked the doors, and headed home, glancing back through the rear view mirror to see if anyone emerged from the nearby bushes. No one appeared.

Within an hour she held her glass of wine and relaxed in the large claw-footed tub. She'd turned on some soft country tunes and sat back, luxuriating in the hot bath as the scents of vanilla and spice floated around her. Lainey closed her eyes and tried to clear her mind. She'd always had a difficult time relaxing. The ability others had to close off their thoughts and enjoy the moment had somehow evaded her. She took a sip of wine and slid back down into the tub as a soft tapping began toward the front of the house.

Lainey sat up, listening to see if the sound came again. A few seconds later, she heard it once more—like someone tapping on a window. She grabbed a towel, wrapped it securely in place, then slid into her robe before walking toward the living room. She looked through the small window in the door, and seeing no one, pushed the door open. A piece of paper fell to the ground.

She grabbed the paper and walked the few feet to the porch steps, and again, saw no one. The street seemed eerily quiet, no people, cars, or bikes. Lainey dashed back inside and unfolded the note to see four typed words—*You're not welcome here.*

Lainey read it again, confused by the message. Was it a threat? A warning? She sat down and stared at the paper once more and wondered if the writer referred to her or Helen, the previous owner. She couldn't imagine anyone having a grudge against Helen, and couldn't think of a single person she might have angered during her brief time in Fire Mountain.

She dropped the note on the dining room table before walking to her bedroom to dress, considering whether or not to take the note to the SAR office the following morning. Perhaps it had to do with her search and rescue involvement. Maybe others had received the same thing, or perhaps it was some type of joke the team pulled on all new volunteers. Regardless, she wouldn't let some prank change any of her plans or her growing fondness for her new town.

******

"What did he say?" Annie asked Heath as they sat down for dinner.

"He thanked me. Told me he wouldn't let me down. Of course I wouldn't have offered him the lead position if I thought he wasn't ready." Heath tucked into his meal. Annie insisted on taking over the cooking duties when his long-time cook retired to relocate near her son. He loved everything his wife cooked.

"He'll do what's needed to make the acquisition work, assuming it still makes sense once he goes over everything." Annie set her fork down. "Does he seem all right to you?"

Heath could sense the concern in her voice. "All right about what?"

"I'm not sure. He's been by to talk a couple of times over the last week. Acted like he wanted to chat about something specific, then closed up. I don't believe I've ever seen him quite this reticent to speak with me. It's probably nothing, just a mother's worry."

"Now that you mention it, he did seem preoccupied during the last senior staff meeting. I didn't think much of it at the time, believing he'd been working too hard and in need of a break. That's when I made the decision he'd be the MacLaren representative for this deal. He needs to stretch a little more and this seems like the right opportunity."

"It's what he's always worked toward. He's much like his father—smart, driven, and dedicated. For that matter, he's a lot like you." Annie smiled and placed her hand on top of Heath's.

"Well, that can be good and bad. Look how long it took me to find you."

******

"How's it going? Are you finding any deal killers?" Eric juggled a load of binders in one hand while trying not to spill a cup of coffee in the other as he hurried to his Monday morning meeting.

"No deal killers yet. It's a clean operation without a single red flag that I can find." Cam held his cell phone between his ear and shoulder as he scribbled some notes on a pad and walked outside to meet Damon Heitz for a lunch appointment. "What's happening there?"

"Not much. Heath's looking at another acquisition. This one in Montana, somewhere near Missoula. They raise bulls for the rodeo circuit."

"He wants to expand into bulls now?"

"Heath wants to expand into anything that makes sense and meshes with what we already have going. He figures the one up north, plus the one you're looking at that supplies bronc riding stock, will round out his plans for the foreseeable future."

"Right. I doubt a day doesn't go by that Heath isn't looking for some new way to expand his operations."

"Agreed. Look, I've just gotten to my meeting. Let's touch base tonight after you get back to your hotel. There are a couple of things I want to talk over with you."

"No problem. I'll call you later." Cam climbed into the waiting car. "Where to today, Mr. Heitz?"

"Italian, if that suits you. And stop calling me Mr. Heitz—makes me feel old. Call me Damon from now on." He pulled onto the main road and pointed to an envelope next to him. "Here's the updated information you requested. Future orders, terms, buyer contacts. We can review it during lunch. I have to tell you, if this does go through, at some point Heath will need to identify a new company president to replace Tom Flint who will be retiring in a couple of years."

Cam had worked with Tom several times during his trip and was disappointed to learn the experienced executive would be leaving. He'd be hard to replace.

"No rush," Damon continued. "Just something to consider. Also, you'll need to identify someone to replace Sonny Burrows as your rodeo contact. He's talked about retiring in a few years, and this time I believe he'll set a firm date. It won't be until his last kid graduates from college, two to three years out. You'll want to identify someone several months in advance so they can travel with Sonny around the country and get to know his contacts."

"Perhaps one of the existing employees could start to train with Sonny."

"Nope. I have a lot of good employees and most have been raised around horses. That's different than what Sonny provides. The person you'll need must already understand the rodeo business and possess existing contacts. It's a competitive business. May be best to get someone who's competed, like Sonny. Contacts are the key in this industry and you need a man who already has them. Again, no rush, just another detail to consider."

******

"Hey, Lainey." Mark stood outside the building that served as the customer center for the small Fire Mountain Airport. It had turned dark as the plane descended and landed on the narrow strip.

Lainey jumped out of her car and ran into Mark's arms. "Hey, yourself." She pulled back and grabbed one of his bags. "I can't believe you did it."

"Most of the time I can't believe it either. I've got to tell you that coming over the mountains and dropping into the valley is a sight I won't forget."

They threw his bags in the back and took off.

"Do you need to stop anywhere before we go to my place?"

"How about I buy you dinner?"

"Perfect. Any place in particular?"

"Basic stuff, nothing fancy."

"I have just the place."

A few minutes later they walked into a sports bar and took seats at a table near one of the big screen televisions.

"What can I get you two?" a spunky waitress in red shorts and striped blouse yelled over the noise of the TV, pool game, and bar conversations.

"Two beers, two burgers with everything, and a large basket of fries." Mark didn't even glance at the menu. He could see what he wanted by looking at the other tables.

"Be back in a jiff." She bounded off toward the kitchen, dodging a couple of patrons, and just missing another waitress holding a full tray of drinks.

"What's on your agenda this week?" Lainey asked as the waitress returned with their beers.

"Megan put me in touch with a realtor. She has six or seven places lined up for me to see tomorrow."

"Do you need my car?"

"Nope. She'll pick me up and drop me back at your place when we're finished. She already told me it takes several days of looking before the right homes start to click. Who knows? Maybe I'll get lucky and find one tomorrow."

"When you do start work?"

"The first of the month, so I have almost three weeks. I'd like to find a place and get it in escrow before I start. So, tell me how it's going for you."

Lainey started to answer before noticing a tall, good looking man walk toward them.

"Hi. Would you be Lainey Devlin?"

"And who wants to know?" Mark chimed in, sizing up the man and wondering what he wanted.

He stuck out his hand. "I'm Eric Sinclair. Jake Renner, over at the bar, pointed you out and I thought I'd welcome both of you to Fire Mountain."

Mark and Lainey glanced behind Eric to see Jake nod at them.

"You wouldn't be related to Cameron Sinclair, would you?" Mark stood and shook Eric's hand.

"Yes, but I hope you won't hold that against me."

Lainey grasped his outstretched hand and smiled. "Is his reputation a problem wherever you go?"

Eric chuckled. "Not usually. He's the quiet, hardworking brother. I'm the good times, slide through life one."

Somehow Lainey doubted that.

"I won't hold you up. Just wanted to say hello and hope you come to love this town the way most of us do."

Eric walked back to the bar and took his seat next to Jake.

"What do you think?" Jake asked as he sipped his beer.

"I think Cam would be a fool not to go after her. Unfortunately, he doesn't see it that way." Eric glanced once more over his shoulder then turned back and shook his head. "He's stubborn, that's for sure."

"And you think nothing is going on between them?"

"Not a thing from what he says."

"She seems like a nice lady and will be a real asset to the SAR team. I'm thinking of pairing them up, with Cam as the senior partner. I need to make a decision by Wednesday night."

Eric almost choked on his beer before recovering. He looked at Jake. "I believe that's a fine idea and I'm quite certain Cam will feel the same."

Chapter Ten

"Thanks for the ride. I'll tell you, it's good to be home." Cam grabbed his one bag from the back seat of Eric's truck and started for the door. "I'd better get moving if I'm going to make the SAR meeting tonight." He waved to his brother, then disappeared inside.

Eric sat in his truck a moment, wondering if he should go after Cam to warn him about Jake's plan to pair him up with Lainey. Jake's idea made sense. Cam had over seven years of experience in mountain, urban, and mounted search and rescue. Even though younger than some of the other volunteers, Eric doubted if anyone would object to Cam taking a leadership role if it were offered. The odds were on Cam to take over for Jake someday. All of these factors made him the perfect choice to partner with Lainey—except the fact that Cam had a thing for her. Eric didn't know how serious, but enough that he'd sure like to be a fly on the wall during the meeting tonight.

Eric pulled away, deciding it best to let Cam deal with the announcement in his own way.

******

Cam could hear Jake talking as he pushed open the back door. He checked his watch—twenty minutes late. He wanted to sneak in and hoped Jake didn't spot him before he took a seat at the back.

"Well, it's good to see Mr. Sinclair decided to join us tonight. I trust you had a good trip to Colorado?"

"Great trip. Glad to be home." Cam grabbed coffee then found a chair. Before he could sit down, Jake called his name.

"Don't bother sitting, Cam. I had just started to give everyone their new partner assignments when you walked in, and you're the first on my list." Jake looked at his notes. "We all know we have two new members—Mark Hill and Lainey Devlin. As is custom, we partner new volunteers, no matter their experience level, with a local team member."

Lainey sat next to Mark and cast him a nervous look. The wariness overshadowed the calm she tried to plaster on her face. She'd hoped to be partnered with Mark, now it appeared she'd be with a local. *Please, do not let it be Cam*, she thought and sat deeper into her seat.

"Cam, you'll be partnered with Lainey. Mark, your partner is Tony Moretti. Please meet up afterwards and set up a training schedule to start by next week."

Lainey couldn't move. The rest of Jake's words had faded after she'd heard her name and Cam's in the same sentence.

"Hey," Mark jostled her leg to get her attention then leaned close. "You want me to see if I can make a switch?"

She glanced at Jake then over to Mark. "No. That's my assignment and I'll do what anyone else would—accept it," she whispered. The resolve in her voice surprised

Lainey. She sure didn't feel as resolute as her words made it sound.

Cam stood up to top off his coffee, irritation bubbling inside him. He didn't have time to tutor a new volunteer and most certainly not Lainey. Hell, he'd be lucky if she even spoke to him. It wouldn't be a surprise if she talked with Jake after the meeting and asked for another partner, or even if Mark could pair up with Cam, and she with Tony.

He'd welcome the switch. The deal in Colorado seemed pretty solid and that meant he'd be traveling back and forth for a while, working with the transition team, perhaps temporarily living in Cold Creek. The assignment meant a great deal to Heath and even more to Cam. It was a chance he couldn't blow, and working with Lainey a couple of times a week would be a distraction he couldn't afford. No matter what she felt about him, his feelings for her had increased with each passing day. He thought he'd gotten himself under control enough to see her and not feel a sense of loss or wanting—neither of which made any sense. Not one damn thing about her made sense.

Cam hadn't been prepared for his body's reaction to seeing her sitting near the front, focused on Jake's every word. His body clenched as a knot rose in his throat, making it damned hard to keep up a façade of indifference. He'd been unprepared and frustrated at how he felt.

If she didn't talk with Jake, he would.

"All right, that's it for tonight. I'll hang around another few minutes if anyone has questions." Jake folded up his notes and shoved them into his shirt pocket.

"Good meeting, Jake."

"Thanks, Frank. Everyone seems fine with the changes. It's good to mix things up once in a while." He looked around the room and spotted Mark, speaking with Tony, and Lainey wandering toward the back, heading in the opposite direction of where Cam sat staring in her direction. Jake thought it had been a smart move to pair the two together—perhaps he'd been wrong. Too late now.

Cam tossed his empty cup in the trash and took a deep breath. Lainey hadn't walked up to speak with Jake as Cam had hoped. The minute the meeting had adjourned, she'd headed toward the back, avoiding the corner where he sat, and making no pretense of her desire to avoid him.

He watched for a few minutes as she spoke to a couple of other female volunteers then slipped past them into the ladies room. Cam guessed he'd just have to wait her out.

Lainey placed her purse on a hook, turned on the faucet, and scrubbed her hands. It had turned into a habit. Working in a preschool meant washing your hands more than a dozen times a day. Tonight, however, it had turned into an excuse to not have to face Cam. They hadn't seen each other in almost three weeks, and no matter what she'd told him, Lainey knew the emotions she held toward Cam had done nothing except increase over time. She looked in the mirror, surprised to see a serene face—not at all reflective of what she felt inside.

Lainey grabbed her bag and pushed through the door into the meeting room. Almost everyone had left. Mark and Tony still chatted in one corner, Mark tapping something into his cell phone and nodding. She glanced around to see no sign of Cam. Good, he'd left.

"Lainey?"

She jumped at the sound of his deep voice then turned to see Cam standing behind her.

"Sorry, I didn't mean to startle you." He stood with his hands in his pockets, his face impassive. "Guess we'd better set something up."

He looked as thrilled about the assignment as she did.

"You know, maybe I could talk with Jake. See if there's someone else who can initiate me into the group."

"You can do that, if that's what you want. I won't stop you."

For some reason Cam's response made her feel worse. He'd now made it obvious he had no desire to be anywhere close to her and would welcome a switch.

Lainey cleared her throat, determined not to let him see how his comment had affected her. "Sure, no problem. I'll see if I can catch him." She took a look around the room, then dashed outside. Four cars were left but she didn't see the big SUV Jake drove. She felt someone walk up beside her, and glanced over to see Cam. "He's gone."

"I'm not surprised. His wife is quite ill and he has a couple of kids at home. The man juggles a lot." Cam's voice remained steady, without a hint of the turmoil he felt. "Look, I just got back from a hectic business trip. Let's sleep on it overnight before making a decision about approaching Jake. I'm sure he has his reasons for pairing us up, and even though neither of us wants to work with the other, it may be best to get the assignment over with and then request new partners."

Cam may as well have slapped her. She could feel her face redden as her temper began to flare. "Wow. I guess there's no doubt how you feel about me and my skills." She brushed a strand of hair away from her eyes and glared up at him. "I don't need to sleep on it. I'll get in touch with Jake tomorrow and request a change." Lainey wasted no time turning toward her car and climbing inside, her heart racing faster with each step. She threw her purse on the seat and started the engine, forgetting about Mark until she saw him walk out the back door with Tony. She'd been too irritated to notice Cam standing outside her window, tapping on the glass. Exasperated, she rolled it down. "What?"

Cam almost jumped back at the irritation in her voice. "Look, Lainey, I'm trying to make the most of an awkward situation and it's obvious I failed. Your skills or experience aren't in question. I just feel with my schedule, and the way things are between us, another partner would suit you better."

Her jaw clenched as she watched him try to reclaim something that had already fallen down a deep, black hole. What an idiot she'd been for thinking this man was something special.

"I'll speak to Jake about finding me someone else. Consider yourself released from your obligation." She rolled up the window as Mark climbed in, his furrowed brow signaling his confusion at the conversation he'd overheard. She slammed the car into reverse and headed home, taking deep breaths, and cursing herself for letting her temper flare.

"Are you going to tell me what just happened?"

She pounded the steering wheel with both hands, then gripped it tight. "He refuses to be my partner and wants me to find someone else."

"He told you that?"

She thought a moment. "Not exactly, but close enough." Lainey made the turn toward her house then rethought it. "How about a drink?"

Mark stared at her. Lainey would have a glass of wine after work or at dinner, a beer with burgers or pizza. He'd never seen her drink out of frustration or anger.

"I'm happy to oblige if you're sure that's what you want."

"Truth is, I don't know what I want, except I'm too agitated to go home to bed. Maybe coffee?"

"With Baileys?"

"You're on."

******

Cam watched as Lainey and Mark pulled out onto the road, feeling empty inside, confused, and unsure how to make his mistakes right. He'd never messed up like this, had no experience to draw upon, and no one except himself to blame.

Jake's announcement could have gone either way as far as Cam's relationship with Lainey. It may have been the push needed for them to rebuild a friendship, or confirmed they'd never again find common ground. Right now, all Cam wanted was a chance to rebuild the relationship they'd started and he'd unintentionally ended.

He trudged to his truck on weary legs, tired clean through, and in need of sleep. There'd be no answers tonight. Cam slid into his truck as his phone rang. He checked caller ID and answered the call.

"What's up?" Cam leaned his head against the seat and closed his eyes.

Eric knew his brother was bone tired and likely frustrated after the SAR meeting. He hated springing this on him tonight. "Mom had an accident."

Cam sat straight up, now wide awake and squeezing the phone tight in his hand. "Where is she?"

"In the hospital. Room 500, top floor. I'm just pulling into the parking lot."

Cam clicked off and headed for Mountain Peak Hospital, unable to focus on anything except seeing his mother. Eric hadn't said what happened or how bad, yet the fact they were keeping her in the hospital told Cam it wasn't good.

He pressed the elevator button to the fifth floor, trying to clear his mind, and relax. He slid through the doors as they began to open, stopping at the nurses' station.

"Annie MacLaren's room. I'm her son." he called to the lady behind the counter.

"Down the hall. It's the corner room on the left."

His long strides propelled him to her room in seconds. He stopped and took a deep breath before opening the door a crack and peering inside. Heath sat next to Annie, holding her hand, and talking in low tones. Eric sat on the opposite side, leaning forward, never letting his eyes leave his mother. Both men looked up as Cam appeared.

"Cam," Heath stood and looked down at his wife. "I'll be right back." He nodded for Cam to follow him into the hallway. "Annie was hit by a drunk driver on her way home from a meeting downtown. She has a broken hip, fractured arm and wrist, concussion, and a lot of bruises. The doctors say she's lucky as they can't find any internal injuries. They've got her on heavy medications, and, of course, want to keep her for several days." Heath's words were heavy, laced with guilt, as if he felt somehow responsible. "The police have the guy in custody."

Cam listened, saying nothing, his stomach twisted as he listened to the list of injuries his mother sustained. "She had plans to fly out to see Brooke in a few days. I guess I should call her—let her know Mom's not coming." His voice broke on the last words, and Heath gripped his shoulder.

"Eric already spoke with Brooke. She's on her way out—didn't want to wait for our plane. You need to go in and see your mother, I just thought you should know what to expect."

Cam nodded and walked past Heath.

"She's going to make it through this, Cam, we all are. Your mother is the strongest woman I know."

Chapter Eleven

"Hello, is Jake at home?" Lainey sat at her desk at the preschool, trying to reach Jake before she left for home. Before she spoke with Cam, she'd wanted to confirm he hadn't already spoken with Jake and requested a different assignment.

"No, he's at the hospital. May I take a message?"

"At the hospital? I hope everything's all right."

"A good friend was hit by a drunk driver last night. Jake's with the family. I doubt he'll be too late. I expect there won't be much space in Annie's hospital room with all the MacLarens around to keep watch on her."

"Would that be Annie Sinclair MacLaren?" Lainey stood at the news about Cam's mother.

"Yes, it is. If you'll give me your name I'll make certain Jake sees it."

"Uh, no, that won't be necessary. I'll get in touch with him another time. Thank you." Lainey hung up, wondering about Cam, and if she could do anything to help. It seemed doubtful.

She'd tried to reach him that morning and hadn't heard back. Now she knew why.

Her suggestion of coffee the night before with Mark had turned into a three-hour discussion—about Mark's new partnership, her business, and, finally, Cam.

"You know, Megan and I've spoken a few times the last three weeks about the partnership, my role, and changes at the firm." Mark stopped to savor his coffee with Bailey's and take a sip. "At one point I mentioned that I'd enjoyed meeting her boyfriend. She told me they'd split up. Megan said both were fine with the decision—no hard feelings either way."

Lainey had thought over Mark's comments the following morning and decided to call Cam, find out if he'd still consider partnering with her. Not many people had the experience he did in several types of rescue situations. The opportunity to work and learn from him might not come again, and she hated to throw away the chance.

Even though he'd split with Megan, Lainey knew the opportunity for anything more with Cam wasn't possible. If he'd told her about Megan up front, let her know he'd planned to end it with his current girlfriend, she might feel differently—he'd chosen not to. Besides, he hadn't hidden his feelings about Jake's request that they partner. Cam had wanted no part of it or her.

Lainey grabbed her keys and started for the door, then stopped and pulled out her phone. She called his number and left a brief message.

"Hi, Cam. It's Lainey. I just heard about your mother. I won't bother you, just want you to know my prayers are with you, and hoping all will turn out well. Call when you have time. I haven't spoken with Jake." She clicked off and slid the phone back in her purse.

Mark had plans for dinner with Megan and Zell that night, so after a brief stop at the store, Lainey drove home. She lifted the grocery sack and started toward the house, noticing a piece of paper wedged between the front door and frame. It fell to the ground as she opened the door. Lainey bent down to pick it up, then paused. The size and color of the paper looked familiar. She snatched it up and unfolded the note.

You're being watched.

A chill passed through Lainey. This time she knew the message was directed at her and not Helen. She crushed the note in her hand and stormed into the house, dropping the bag and her purse on the counter before pulling out her phone.

"Search and Rescue."

"Hi Frank. It's Lainey."

"Hey, Lainey. What do you need?"

"I just found a note at my front door and wondered if any of the team might be playing some type of prank on me. An initiation thing or something?"

Frank's tone grew serious. "Not a chance. Jake won't put up with any of that hazing stuff. Why?"

"It's probably nothing, just a note someone left saying they were watching me. Must be some of the neighborhood kids."

"Read it to me."

Lainey read the three words out loud, the full meaning beginning to sink in.

"Doesn't sound good. If you're not sure it's a prank, call the police. At least let them know. It's the first note, right?"

"No, the second."

"Don't mess around. Call the police and let them know. Tonight."

"I'm not sure..."

"If you don't, I will." Frank's stern tone told Lainey he meant what he said.

"I hear you, Frank. I'll take care of it."

"Let me know if you get another one of those notes."

They hung up, Lainey unsure of her next move. She didn't want to overreact if it turned out to be a prank from a neighborhood kid. She knew Frank would contact the police if he found out she hadn't. Mark had flown back to Idaho that morning to pack his things. Maybe she'd call him, then decide.

******

Cam felt the phone vibrate in his pocket as he walked into his mother's room and closed the door. He glanced at the caller ID—Lainey. She'd have to wait. Just one day had passed since the accident, if one could call it that, and already Annie looked much better.

"Hey, Mom." Cam pulled a chair next to the bed, spun it around, and straddled it, resting his arms on the back. "How are you feeling tonight?"

"Much better than last night. Hope to go home tomorrow." Annie's groggy voice sounded raspier than it did earlier in the day.

"Tomorrow, huh? Is that what the doctor said?"

"Not exactly. A woman can hope you know."

Cam looked over his shoulder when he heard the door open and Eric walked in. He walked to the other side of the bed and leaned over to place a kiss on his mother's cheek.

"How you feeling, Mom?"

"Going home tomorrow." Annie glanced at Cam, daring him to contradict her.

"Right." Eric smirked and sat down across from Cam. "What did the doctor say today?"

Cam helped her sit up and take a sip of water.

"He says I've improved since yesterday—doing better than he expected given the extent of the injuries."

"At least they confirmed no internal injuries. Your bones will heal, at least mine did." Eric's voice sounded flat, concerned.

"She's just trying to outdo you, Eric." All eyes turned to the door at the sound of Heath's deep voice. "I'm beginning to think the Sinclair branch of the family has bad karma when it comes to motorized vehicles," Heath joked as he kissed his wife and stroked a finger down her cheek.

"Hey, don't include me in that statement," Cam objected.

"It wasn't my fault some idiot driver ran my bike off the road," Eric replied.

"With you on it," Cam added.

Eric grimaced, remembering his sorry state after the accident on his motorcycle over a year ago. "Is Doctor Newcastle your orthopedist?"

"Possibly, but not if Heath has any say it in," Annie smiled. She'd been dating Barry Newcastle when her relationship with Heath changed.

"I don't fault Barry for his interest in you, Annie. Anyway, he lost, I won." Heath leaned against the wall, his arms crossed, looking self-satisfied. Unfortunately, even his cocky stance didn't diminish the worry in his eyes. He'd practically been living at the hospital since Annie's accident and his weariness showed.

"You have to admit, he did a great job. I'm good as new." Eric stood to emphasize the complete recovery of his broken leg.

They turned at the knock on Annie's door. Heath walked over and pulled it open.

"Hello, Jake. Good to see you. Come on in."

Jake slipped past Heath, and stood at the end of the bed, a small vase in his hand.

"Hi, Annie. How're you doing?"

"Much better tonight, Jake. Are those for me?"

"Emma reminded me how much you like plants." His sheepish reply had the men grinning.

Heath took the vase from Jake and clasped his shoulder. "How's Emma doing?"

"Still in remission. She's weak most of the time, but wants to go back to work soon. We're hoping for the best." He turned back to Annie. "When are you getting out of here?"

"Tomorrow, assuming the doctor will listen to me."

The group fell into quiet conversations while Heath left to speak with the nurse, Eric discussing his physical therapy experiences, and Cam talking about the last SAR meeting with Jake.

"I know you've been swamped, Cam. Did you already schedule the first training session with Lainey or would it be best if I found someone else?"

Cam sat forward, resting his arms on his knees before looking back up at Jake.

"We didn't have a chance to pick a date. She planned to call today." That's when Cam remembered the other call earlier that day. The second one from her he'd ignored. "Give me a day or so to see if Lainey and I can work something out."

"Cam, don't be changing your schedule on my account." Annie had heard enough of the conversation to understand Cam's reluctance might be due to her accident. "I have plenty of help. Do what you have to."

Eric sat back, watching and wondering if Cam still struggled with his attraction to Lainey. No matter how much Cam might deny it, Eric knew his brother had feelings for her—strong ones.

Cam glanced at his mother, then to Jake. "I'll work it out with Lainey. Don't worry about it."

"All right." Jake stood and put his hand over Annie's. "Sure hope you're able to go home tomorrow. I know what it's like living in a hospital room. Call if you need anything." He squeezed her hand lightly then turned to leave as Heath walked back into the room. "I'm heading home, Heath. Let me know if I can help in any way."

"I will. You take care." Heath watched Jake start down the hall. "I don't know how he does it. Emma's illness, the kids, his job, and SAR. He must run on adrenaline." He shook his head and looked back toward Annie. "The doctor will be here in about ten minutes."

"You found that out from the pretty nurse you used to date?"

Heath's eyes snapped to his wife's. "You knew about that?"

Annie smiled as Cam and Eric tried to stifle grins. "Heath MacLaren, it would be easier to list the women you didn't date before me." She laughed for the first time since her accident, making it impossible for Heath not to join in.

"You have a point there."

******

Cam slipped into his truck a couple of hours later, starving and ready for bed. At least he knew his mother would be going home in two or three more days. She hadn't been happy about the delay, but kept her disappointment to herself.

He pulled out his phone and called a local Chinese take-out place, ordered, then started to toss the phone on the seat when he remembered to check his messages. A couple from his office, neither urgent, one from Eric telling him he was on his way to the hospital, he erased it, and another message from Lainey. He supposed he'd better call her back.

Lainey had just turned off the light and snuggled under the covers when she heard her phone. She thought briefly about not answering, just staying tucked in her warm bed, then remembered the message she'd left for Cam.

"Hello."

"Lainey, it's Cam."

She wasn't prepared for the immediate and intense sensation that flowed through her at the sound of his voice. She could listen to his voice all day long and never tire of the sound—deep, rich, and sensual.

"Lainey, you there?"

"Um, yes, I'm here."

"Sorry to call so late but I just left the hospital."

"I heard about the accident. I'm so sorry. How is your mother?"

"Better. Ready to come home. The doctor may release her in a couple of days, assuming she keeps improving. Not much anyone can do except wait until he makes a decision. Hold on a moment."

Lainey could hear rustling through the phone.

"Sorry. I haven't had anything to eat since breakfast so I grabbed some take out."

"Where are you?"

He looked through his window. "Next to Mountain Elementary."

"Cam, you're two blocks from my place. Come on over here and eat, I'll give you a beer and we can talk." She gave him her address.

"I'll be there in five minutes."

It took just two before he parked in front of her house, an old Victorian with a wraparound porch. He could see her red SUV parked in the drive. For a moment he thought he glimpsed a shadow or silhouette on the driver's side but dismissed it as a symptom of his exhaustion. Cam grabbed the sack and climbed up the porch steps as Lainey opened the door.

The first sight of her since their argument a few nights before caused Cam to stop and stare. She wore loose fitting draw-string pants with a white tank top and her feet were bare. Her hair was slightly disheveled as if she'd just run her fingers through it. Cam got the sudden urge to pull her to him and do the same—slide his hands through her hair, down her back, and mold her body to his.

"Well, you don't need to stand there. Come on in." Lainey held the door open. "How about a beer to go with…"

"Chinese. There's plenty. We can share."

"I'll grab chop sticks."

Within minutes they were digging into Kung Pao chicken, Mongolian beef, fried rice, and a mixture of vegetables and noodles.

"You bought enough for an army," Lainey commented as she stabbed some beef with her chop sticks.

"Like I said, I was starving."

They ate in silence for a while, neither knowing quite how to approach the subject that had caused such intense reactions earlier in the week, and neither willing to chance a repeat of that night.

Lainey took a last bite then cleared her throat. "About us pairing up. I've been thinking about it, and if you're willing to try it, so am I."

Relief seemed mild compared to the feeling that overtook Cam at Lainey's words. She'd made it simple, no drama or excuses, just a professional willingness to work through their differences and move forward. "I'd like that."

"Great. I know you're busy with all that's going on, so you tell me what works best."

"Saturday okay with you?"

"Perfect."

"We'll meet at SAR and go from there. Eight o'clock." He checked his watch, reluctant to leave but knowing he had no choice. "Guess I better head out."

She walked him to the door. "Thanks."

He turned at her words. "For what?"

"Your willingness to work with me after what I said the other night."

"It was as much my doing as yours. We'll forget it and move on."

Lainey put her hand on the knob when they heard a loud crash from the back of the house.

"What the hell was that?" Cam said and took off down the hall, Lainey right behind.

He opened the door to one room, and seeing nothing, stepped to the next door, the laundry room. "Shit." He knelt beside the back door, the one that used to have glass framed in the upper half. Cam looked to the side of the clothes dryer and found a rock about two inches in diameter lying amid a sea of broken glass. He picked it up and held it out to Lainey. "You having problems with the neighbors?"

She stared at the rock and glass, feeling angry, confused, and vulnerable. "I don't know who would've done this. There's the older couple next door, and a couple with children on the other side. They're the only ones I've met." She took the rock from Cam and turned it in her hand. "It sure did a lot of damage."

The words had just left her lips when another crash came from the front. Lainey turned, ready to run back toward the living room when Cam grabbed her arm.

"You stay here. I'll let you know what I find."

"But..."

"Stay here, please. I'll check it out."

She stiffened, not liking the way he ordered her to fall back. Lainey decided to give Cam one minute, then follow him. Her front door opened and closed, then opened once more. She headed to the front.

"I can't see anyone outside, but you need to look at this." He held a small block of wood in his hand, a string securing an envelope in place.

Lainey took it, pulled the envelope free, and tore it open. Her eyes widened as she stared at the message. She glanced up at Cam, then back at the note.

"What's it say?"

She held the paper out for Cam to read.

You don't belong here. Leave before someone gets hurt.

Cam's anger rose as he read the message a second time. He placed a finger under Lainey's chin and lifted her face to him. "You want to tell me what this is about?"

Chapter Twelve

Lainey stared up at him, a knot forming in her stomach, as the need to run out of the house and track the assailant down overcame her. She started to turn toward the front door when Cam restrained her with a hand to her arm.

"This house belongs to me, it means something, and I'll not let anyone force me out with continued threats." She clenched her hands and took a deep breath.

"Sit down a minute, we can clean this up later." He took Lainey's arm and escorted her to the sofa in the living room, then sat next to her. "Now, you're going to tell me what's going on." Cam's hard-edged tone told her he wouldn't leave until he knew what was happening.

"Let me get something from the bedroom." She dashed upstairs, grabbed the other notes, and made her way back to Cam, holding out the previous threats.

He read each before setting them on a nearby table, his face a mask, lips pursed. The rage Cam felt at the threats to Lainey surprised him. He wanted to find the person responsible and tear them apart, make them pay for scaring the woman he...what? Loved, wanted? What did he feel toward this woman?

"Who else knows of this?"

"Just Frank. I thought it might be a prank, you know, hazing the new person. He told me Jake doesn't allow such behavior. The first two were wedged in the front door, there wasn't any damage."

"What else did Frank say?"

"He told me to call the police. He said if I didn't call them, he would."

"So what did the police say?" He already knew the answer, but needed to hear her say it.

"I didn't call them."

"Shit," Cam mumbled and scrubbed a hand over his face before pulling out his phone and punching in a number.

"What are you doing?"

"What you should've done after the first note. I'm calling the police."

"But..." her words trailed off when his eyes, radiating of barely controlled fury, narrowed on hers.

"Is Sergeant Towers working tonight?" Cam paused a moment. "Yes, I'll hold."

"You know him?"

Cam nodded, then focused back on the call. "Hi, Buck." He listened a moment. "She's doing better, thanks. I'm just glad they arrested the person who did it. But look, there's a situation at a friend's house. Lainey Devlin." Cam gave Buck the address. "Vandalism, threats." He paused again. "Three notes. Good. I'll be here when you arrive."

"Guess I'd better clean up this mess."

"No. Don't touch anything. Buck and his men will want to see the damage, check outside, and probably take the notes. Why don't you get us some coffee while we wait?"

"You don't have to stay. I can handle it."

"I'm staying."

Five minutes later, Cam could hear Buck's squad car pull into the driveway behind Lainey as another parked behind his truck. He opened the door to three officers and held out his hand to Buck.

"Thanks for getting here so fast." He nodded to Lainey. "Buck, this is Lainey Devlin. She owns the house."

"Nice meeting you, Ms. Devlin. Why don't you show me the notes first, then the damage, while you explain what happened?"

Cam grabbed the notes from the living room. "There are three. The one tonight was wrapped around a block of wood that was thrown through the window over there." Cam motioned to the shattered front window.

"When did you get these other two, Ms. Devlin?"

"Over the last couple of weeks. Each had been wedged into the front door and frame. I couldn't see any damage. The first time I heard tapping on the front window. I went to check it out, saw nothing, and opened the front door. That's when I saw the note drop to the ground."

Buck scribbled in his notebook while the other officers took pictures of the damage and checked outside for anything that might help them figure out what happened. "And the second note?"

"I heard noise from the front and went to check it out. I didn't see anyone through the front door glass, so I stepped outside to look up and down the street. There weren't any people or moving cars. As I turned back inside, I saw the note on the porch. It must have been stuck between the door and jamb, the same as the other one."

"You didn't call the police, file a report?"

She looked away, feeling foolish for not reporting the two incidents. "No. I did call Frank Moretti at SAR headquarters. I thought it might be a prank they played on new volunteers. He assured me no one with the team would pull something like this." Lainey cleared her throat. "Frank did tell me to contact you. Guess I should have listened to him."

Buck narrowed his eyes at her, but said nothing. "All right, we'll go with what we have. Anyone you can think of who'd have a grudge against you, want you to leave?"

"No one. I just bought a small business and moved into this house. I've met so few people that I can't imagine having already made an enemy. Between my business and SAR, there's been little time for getting involved in the community." She shook her head. "I'm sorry Sergeant. All of this baffles me."

Buck continued to scribble while Lainey spoke. He knew someone had it in for the young woman, she just hadn't taken the time to sort through all the possibilities. Vandalism escalated the threats to a new level, one that would require her to search her contacts and acquaintances for anyone who might hold a grudge against her.

"I want you to think through everything since you arrived in town. Everyone you've met or interacted with, not leaving anyone out. It may have to do with something you haven't thought of, something minor. You'd be surprised at how something you consider minor can be elevated to a level another person considers more serious—knocking into someone with your grocery cart, cutting off a car in traffic. Remember, we're not dealing with a person who is rational. Few people send threatening notes and vandalize—for any reason. What you're experiencing is extreme and potentially more serious than I believe you realize." He closed the notebook and glanced around the room once more. "Do you have someplace to stay tonight?"

"Just here."

"She can stay at my place," Cam offered, not turning his eyes toward Lainey.

"Absolutely not. I won't let someone push me out of my home."

"The truth is, someone has threatened you, Ms. Devlin, broken into your house and caused a good deal of damage. I agree with Cam. Stay with him, or someplace else."

Lainey swept her gaze around the living room. The damage did seem more extensive than she'd first thought. One full window had been broken, with glass strewn across the floor as far as the dining room.

"Look, you stay at my place, or I stay here. Either works for me." Cam's stern expression indicated he'd sleep in his car if needed.

Lainey's glare told Cam just what she thought of his idea, but kept her thoughts to herself.

She crossed her arms and stared at him. "Fine, you can stay in my guest room."

"Glad you got that settled." Buck glanced between the two, then focused on Lainey. "I want to meet with you tomorrow, here or the station, whatever works for you. That'll give you time to think through all the contacts you've made. I want to know everything you've done since arriving. All right?"

"That's fine. I'll write down as much as I can remember. Will after work be soon enough? I run a preschool. There's no way I can cancel tomorrow at this point."

"What time?"

"Six o'clock."

Buck nodded and stretched his hand out to Lainey then to Cam. "Sorry to meet you under these circumstances, Ms. Devlin. This is normally a quiet town, good people, and little trouble. We'll find out who's behind this and stop them."

Sergeant Towers walked out the door, leaving Lainey and Cam to clean up the damage. Cam began in the front room while Lainey cleaned up the laundry.

"Do you have any cardboard or scrap wood we can place over the broken glass?" Cam dumped the last of the broken shards in the trash can.

"There's a storage shed out back. I'll go check." She started toward the kitchen door, stopping when Cam grabbed her arm.

"Let me go. I'll see what you have and bring it inside."

"You can come with me, but I'm going." She pushed on through the opening, leaving him to follow close behind. A part of her was glad at his offer to stay and help, another part felt crowded. She wasn't used to anyone hovering the way he seemed to be doing. An image of Robert flashed through her mind. She knew he would have walked out with the Sergeant and driven home, an offer to help clean up would have never entered his mind. He still left messages and sent emails, all of which she ignored. Lainey supposed it would be wise to respond, except something held her back.

"Where's Mark? I thought he was staying with you until he found a place." Cam stopped beside Lainey as she slid the key into a lock on the shed door, and noticed how old the wooden structure appeared. He guessed it had been built at the same time as the house.

"Mark found a house the first week. He flew back to Bluebird Falls to pack his furniture and clothes. There's enough to fit into a small moving van. I expect he'll be back early next week."

She pulled the door open and let Cam walk past her to the inside.

"All this stuff yours?" Old garden equipment, tools, buckets, and various bags of seeds and fertilizer filled the shed.

"Only the bicycle. Helen left the rest when she moved."

He looked around the area. "I don't see anything that will work. Let's head out to SAR headquarters. There are several boxes cut down and stored there. Those should be perfect for covering the broken windows. Tomorrow we'll get someone out to replace them."

"I can't leave the place like it is." Lainey gestured toward the house. They could see the broken laundry room window from where they stood.

"Someone would need to break more glass and push through the window trim to enter either room. Besides, I doubt anyone will be back tonight—especially if they saw the police cars." He pulled out his keys. "We'll take my truck."

******

They rode in silence to the SAR office, Lainey's hands clasped in her lap, her mind working double-time to sort through the threats. Like most people, she'd never been involved in anything like this before and had no experience dealing with intimidation.

"What about Bluebird Falls?" Cam's voice broke through the silence.

Lainey turned her head. "Bluebird Falls?"

"Anybody there ever threaten you? Could be something from the past has surfaced here."

She thought a moment, letting her mind leaf through the people she'd known in Idaho. "No one. I can't think of anybody, there or here, who would do something like this to me."

"Buck's right, you need some time to clear your head, think of everyone you know and not dismiss them right off." He parked and slid out. "Why don't you stay here? It'll just take me a minute to grab the boxes."

She rested her head against the seat back and closed her eyes. She'd been involved in just two difficult situations in the last few months—her breakup with Robert and the incident with the little girl she'd found near Golden Lake. Lainey felt certain Robert would never be involved in threats or vandalism. Even though he hadn't stopped emailing and his voice messages had become more urgent and emotional, she knew he wouldn't do anything that could interfere with his career or reputation.

The little girl had been returned to her grandmother. Lainey never met the father and thought it doubtful he even knew her identity. His anger would be directed toward the grandmother, the woman who'd been declared his daughter's legal guardian.

She jumped at the sound of the door opening. Cam climbed in and started the engine, eyeing her pensive expression and startled gaze. "Are you all right?"

"I'm fine. Just trying to figure out who'd do these things. You may be right. I'll sleep on it and hope something comes to mind in the morning."

Lainey settled back in her seat as Cam pulled out his phone.

"Eric? Hi, it's Cam. Look, I need you to swing by my place in the morning. Grab a clean shirt, tie, and jacket."

"Where are you?" Eric's groggy voice told Cam he'd woken up his brother.

"I'll explain tomorrow. Just bring them to the office. I'll be there by eight." Cam ended the call before Eric could ask any more questions.

"Your brother?"

"Eric. He works for our stepfather also."

"I know. I met him not long ago when Mark and I went out for burgers. Nice guy."

"He's too young for you." The words were out of Cam's mouth before he realized what he'd said.

Lainey cocked a brow, her eyes glittering. "Too young?"

Cam thought he saw the hint of a smile curve her lips. "Yes, too young," he repeated with firm emphasis. He gripped the steering wheel and focused straight ahead, hoping she would let his comment stand.

"You mentioned the other night that you'd been out of town. Colorado, right?"

"Heath asked me to lead the evaluation effort for a potential new acquisition. It's something I've strived to do for years and I don't plan to let the family down." His resolute voice told Lainey how serious he took his job and duty to the family.

"My impression is you rarely, if ever, let anyone down. Have you ever failed at anything, Cam? I mean, something that made an immediate negative impact in your life?"

His gaze swung to her before focusing back on the road. "Yes."

Lainey waited before comprehending he didn't plan to elaborate. "Care to share it with me?"

She could see his jaw tighten as if struggling for an answer.

"Maybe another time."

Cam rounded the corner onto Lainey's street as three kids took off running through her driveway. He screeched to a stop, jumped out, and chased them. "Stay there!" he called over his shoulder before disappearing into an alley behind her home.

Lainey slid behind the wheel and pulled the truck into her driveway, keeping the headlights trained on the path Cam took out the back. A few minutes later he emerged, alone, and jogged up to his truck.

"I couldn't catch them." He looked back over his shoulder at the alley then trained his attention on the front porch. "We'd better see if there's any further damage."

They inspected the front then walked around the house, finding nothing had changed since they'd left.

"Probably just curious teenagers." Lainey turned in a circle, trying to spot anything they'd missed. "The police made a lot of commotion when they were here earlier. It's hard to stay away from something like that when you're young."

Cam didn't seem convinced. "Could be. I'll feel better when the damage is fixed and Buck locates the person who vandalized your place." Cam trudged up the back steps as Lainey slipped inside. She had deadbolt locks on all her doors and he checked each one as Lainey made up the guest room, grabbing an extra blanket and bath towels.

"I hope this is comfortable for you. Helen told me it's a new bed."

"I'll be fine. Any bed right now would work for me."

"You already know where the bathroom is. Feel free to grab whatever you want from the kitchen." She grabbed another pillow from the linen closet and slipped on a new cover.

They settled into a tense silence, Cam focusing his gaze on Lainey, while she pretended to fidget with the pillowcase.

"You don't have to stay. I'm sure nothing else will happen tonight." Her reasonable tone was overshadowed by a slight stammer.

"The decision is made. I'm staying. What time do you leave for work?"

"I have to be out of here no later than six thirty."

He took a few steps toward the living room and peeked into each room once more before turning back to Lainey. "Come and get me if you hear anything."

"I will."

He nodded. "All right. I'll see you in the morning."

Cam waited while she trudged up the stairs and turned on her bedroom light. He couldn't help feeling an impending sense of disaster. Nothing about the threats to Lainey felt like a prank. In his mind, whoever left the notes and vandalized her house wanted her gone—permanently—from Fire Mountain. He doubted the threats would stop until either she left or they found the person responsible.

Chapter Thirteen

He'd hidden down the street, behind some bushes a few houses away, surveying the damage and watching as the cops took photos and scribbled in notebooks. This had turned out to be more fun than he'd first thought.

He'd done a few illegal things in his life—fencing stolen electronics, stealing cars for parts, roughing up people when needed, including a man who'd refused to pay a debt. How was he supposed to know the guy had a heart problem? After a few blows to the head and stomach, the guy keeled over and stopped breathing. They'd never pinned the death on him, which heightened his confidence, making him feel as if he'd gotten away with murder—which he had. He'd also sold cocaine a few times to make some quick cash. The couple of crimes they'd busted him for were bogus—he'd done worse, the cops just didn't know it. In comparison, his actions now didn't even seem like a crime.

He just needed to scare her enough to question her reasons for moving to Fire Mountain. It could take days or weeks. None of that mattered. He needed her to be afraid and uncertain. He knew from experience that self-preservation would kick in once her doubts took control, and she'd convince herself the one way to stay safe was to leave Fire Mountain.

He stayed hidden until the last of the two patrol cars drove off, then kept low until he'd reached his older, well-used, dark brown van, and opened the back door. The space overflowed with everything he needed to handle his day-to-day life. Most people thought him weird. In his mind, the items he kept close at hand were required to keep his life ordered.

He felt the vibration before hearing the slight buzzing sound of his phone. Slipping it out of his pocket, he glanced at the ID. His mother.

"Hi, Ma."

"Where are you?" He'd become accustomed to the raspy smoker's voice of his mother. She'd already had part of one lung removed, yet continued her two-pack-a-day habit.

"I told you, Ma. I'm out of town, doing a job."

"When will you be back?" She choked the deep, gurgling sound someone made when they couldn't get a breath.

"A week, maybe longer. Why?"

"Both your ex-wives called looking for their child support. I swear those women must talk to each other. They threatened to take you back to court if they don't get paid this week."

"Shit," he mumbled under his breath, wanting to say more but not wishing to upset his mother. "I'll handle it, Ma. If they call again, tell them I'm on a job and will have the money to them by the middle of the month." He watched as another police car drove slowly down the street. "Look, Ma, I've got to go. I'll call you in a few days." He clicked off and drove out of the area, knowing he'd be back within the next forty-eight hours. The calls from his ex-wives ramped up the need for money. He'd have to speed up his timeline for scaring the pretty preschool teacher. His relaxed timeline had just been upgraded to make this his top priority. If he had to guess, he lay odds she'd be gone within days.

******

"Let's go over any negatives first, Cam. We don't need to dwell on the plusses of the acquisition." Heath pushed from his chair to top off his coffee cup, then settled back down to listen to Cam's report.

"This won't take long. I can't find any red flags that would stop a deal. Cash flow, receivables, cash in the bank, age of equipment, the quality of livestock, and employee loyalty are all solid. His banker did everything but get on his knees in an attempt to explain to me the importance of Damon's business to Cold Creek."

"What will we lose once Damon retires?"

"I don't believe that will be an issue. He's focused on making this deal work. If that means staying one year, two, or three to make sure all his contacts stay with the company, he'll do it." Cam reviewed his notes. "There are two personnel changes that will need attention in the first couple of years, besides Damon, of course. The president of the company has told Damon he wants to retire in a year. He'll stay two if needed, but that's his limit."

"And the other one?"

"The head of rodeo relations plans to leave once his kids are out of college, which is about two years, could be longer."

"Sonny Burrows?"

"That's right. You know him?"

"Hell, everyone who's ever been around a rodeo knows him. The man's won more awards in bronc riding than anyone else. And he held his family together through it all. That in itself is a minor miracle." Heath scrubbed a hand over his jaw. "He'll be hard to replace."

"Damon indicated that none of the current employees could take over for him."

"I don't doubt it. Sonny's friendships and chit barrel run pretty deep."

"Chit barrel?"

Heath chuckled. "The man's got a barrel full of chits he can call in whenever needed. Sonny's a man that repays his debts, cash or otherwise, and knows he can count on others to repay theirs. That's something you don't just pass along to the new guy."

Cam thought a moment. "Too bad Cassie's boyfriend isn't further along in his career. He rides broncs, doesn't he?"

"Matt? The kid just dabbles in it between his coursework at college. He's got the personality, drive, and skill. Unfortunately, he'd have to make it a full-time career for a while to pick up connections like Sonny."

Cassie MacLaren was Heath's daughter, Cam's stepsister. She and her boyfriend, Matt Garner, attended college in Phoenix. Both families thought they'd eventually marry and move back to Fire Mountain, Cassie for a job with the family, and Matt with his grandfather, a long-time MacLaren friend. Fact was, the Garners and MacLarens were some of the most established and respected ranchers in Fire Mountain dating back to the 19th century. Now Seth Garner and his grandkids focused on construction, even though they still kept a decent herd of cows and a couple dozen horses.

"We've got time on that one. If I recall correctly, his kids are younger than Cassie. With luck and the right incentives, we can stretch Sonny's retirement out a few years."

"Higher pay, what?"

"We have a college tuition program for employees and their children. Once he's with MacLaren, Sonny will be eligible for that and other incentives I'm sure he doesn't get now. Plus, he'll have all the autonomy he wants."

"What about the president retiring?"

"Don't worry about that now. I have some ideas." Heath checked his watch. "I'd better get down to Doug's office and go over the latest numbers. That man does enjoy his job," referring to the company's CFO who'd been with Heath since both had graduated from college.

"I'm on my way to meet Brooke at the hospital. You remember the doctor is releasing Mom after lunch today, right?"

"You think your mother would let me forget that? She's called three times today and it's only ten o'clock," he grinned. "I'll meet you guys there."

******

"Yes, Cassie, I'm doing much better. No, don't change your plans. Go have a great time and come up in two weeks. Love you too, honey." Annie set down the phone and glanced over at Heath with a questioning look on her face.

"I heard, and you did right. She and Matt have had plans for weeks to head to the cabin north of Phoenix with friends. You're doing fine, and the truth is, there's nothing she can do for you the rest of us can't." He squeezed her hand. "I better check on the crew. Here," he handed her a cow bell. "Ring this if you need me."

Annie's laughter followed him down the hall. God, it was good to have her home.

Brooke, Cam, and Eric were in the kitchen with Heath's brother, Jace, and his wife, Caroline, preparing supper and planning out a schedule to help Heath while Annie recovered. Caroline and Annie had been close friends long before Caroline introduced her to Heath. He knew he could never repay his sister-in-law for bringing Annie and him together.

"What's for supper?"

"Your chicken enchilada casserole, beans and rice, cornbread, salad, pie, and ice cream. Is that enough?"

Caroline asked as she set a large salad bowl on the counter and piled in various vegetables.

"All that for just us?" Brooke looked at the pile of food and two casserole dishes Jace slipped into the oversized oven.

"So you'll have leftovers," Eric joked as he continued to stir the black beans Caroline had prepared.

"How is she, Heath?" Cam hadn't joined the rest in the friendly banter. His mind moved between his mother, and her still rather fresh injuries, and the threats to Lainey. He just couldn't shake the feeling something worse would happen before Buck identified the person responsible.

"You saw her." Heath studied Cam, seeing more in his eyes than concern for his mother. "Do you want to tell me what else is going on? This isn't just about Annie, is it?"

Cam didn't want to burden Heath with anything else, and wouldn't, except he sure could use someone else's insights into what was going on. "Do we have time before supper?"

"We'll make time. Come on."

Cam followed Heath into his study, and closed the door.

"I've met someone. She's new to town, bought a local preschool, and is part of the SAR team."

"And, Megan?"

"We split a few weeks ago. It's all good. We've been able to remain friends."

Heath nodded for Cam to continue.

Cam slumped into a chair and squeezed the bridge of his nose between his thumb and index finger. "Two things, I guess. The first is I just don't have time for a relationship. There's too much going on and my schedule's already packed." He paused when Heath held out a glass with Scotch, Cam's drink of choice when he had something to figure out. He took a swallow. "The second thing is, well, I can't get her out of my head." Cam slugged back the rest of the light amber liquid and set the glass on Heath's desk.

Heath took a seat next to Cam. "It sounds like you believe you must make a choice. Your career or a woman."

Cam blew out a breath. "I just don't see how I can focus on my work, which I love by the way, and build a new relationship. Megan and I were easy—I knew right off it would never go anywhere."

"This time you believe it could?"

"I'm certain of it." Cam hadn't voiced his belief until that moment. The realization that Lainey could be the one woman for him scared the hell out of him.

"Then there doesn't need to be a choice. If she's the right one, she'll understand the demands of your career, just as you'll understand her commitments as the owner of a preschool. You'll both have to compromise if you want a relationship to work. Don't misunderstand, you're needed in the business. There's a lot going on you and Eric don't know about that I'm not at liberty to discuss tonight. At the same time, you will be able to find time to have a relationship, perhaps marry, and start a family, if

145

that's what you want. You don't have to settle for one or the other."

Cam stood and walked to the large window that looked toward the mountains. "Dad was gone most of the time." He turned toward Heath. "I don't know if she ever told you, but he'd be gone for weeks on investor trips, scouting out new companies and investment opportunities. That's why Eric, Brooke, and I are so close to Mom. She's all we had most of the time." He shoved his hands in his pockets. "They loved each other, but their life wasn't like yours and Mom's—not even close. The truth is, I want a marriage like the two of you. I don't want to be a husband or father who leaves his family for long stretches to further his career."

Heath stood and took the few steps to stand next to Cam. "If that's what worries you, forget it." He clasped Cam on the shoulder. "I don't expect that of anyone, and neither does Jace. We both have families and that commitment comes before our work. What you need to decide is if she's the one. If so, then you'd be a fool to pass up your chance."

Cam felt relief pass through his body at Heath's words. If Cam had his stepfather's support, he knew he could make it work. "Thanks, Heath. I appreciate it."

"By the way, what's her name?"

"It's Lainey. Lainey Devlin."

******

"Lainey, there's a phone call for you." One of the teachers handed her the phone and took over Lainey's duties in the small, outside play area.

"Ms. Devlin?"

"Yes."

"This is Pete, your next door neighbor. There's a fire at your place."

"My God, is it the house?" Lainey grabbed her purse and sweater.

"Looks like the storage shed. I've called the fire department and they're on their way."

"I'm heading home now. Thanks, Pete." She dashed outside. "There's a fire at my house. Are you okay with the children for a little while?"

"It's already four thirty and there are just five children left. Go. I'm fine."

Lainey sped home, hoping she didn't trigger any speed limit sensors on the way, and praying her house would still be there when she arrived. Lainey could see the commotion from a block away. A police blockade stopped her from getting too close, so she parked and sprinted toward the billowing, black smoke.

"Sorry, ma'am. You'll need to stay back."

"But that's my home..." Lainey's words trailed off when she saw the fire crew working to contain the blaze to the back buildings and not let it jump to her house.

"Ms. Devlin?"

Lainey looked up to see Sergeant Towers standing next to her.

"Come on. Let's let them do their job. You can wait with me over here." He guided her toward his squad car a hundred yards away. "I know you want to be close, but believe me, you want to stay out of their way." He nodded back over his shoulder to the fire crew who scrambled to keep the blaze contained. "Is there someone I can call? Maybe Cam Sinclair?"

Lainey stared, still not believing what she saw right in front of her, and not comprehending the full extent of the danger. The recurring dream she'd had since her parents died in a hotel fire kept playing through her mind. Flames, heat, smoke, and screams, and no one could get away.

"Ms. Devlin. Should I call Cam?"

She glanced at Buck, her eyes filled with confusion and pain, and what Buck would describe later as determination. Lainey nodded, then leaned against the patrol car and continued to watch as the fire crew fought to keep her home from complete destruction.

Chapter Fourteen

"Are you going to stay at Lainey's again tonight?" Eric asked as he, Cam, and Brooke worked in the kitchen, cleaning up while Heath, Jace, and Caroline kept Annie company in the downstairs bedroom that had been outfitted with a special bed, intercom, and rolling tables.

"That's my plan. I'm not comfortable leaving her alone with some lunatic making threats." He placed the last of the glasses in the cupboard and grabbed another pan.

Brooke stacked the dried plates and set them aside. "Who's Lainey? The last I heard you were dating someone named Megan."

"They split. Don't you ever read my emails?" Eric sliced a look at his sister.

"Of course I read them." Brooke leaned against a countertop with her arms crossed.

"Then you'd know Megan's out and Lainey is in."

"Lainey and I are friends, that's all," Cam interjected before Eric got carried away. "She had a scare and Buck Towers, he's with the police department, recommended she not stay alone at the house." Cam started to say more until the sound of his phone interrupted him. "This is Cam."

"It's Buck Towers. There's a fire at Lainey's—"

"What? Where is she?" Cam threw the dish towel at Eric as he dashed toward the door.

"She wasn't in the house, Cam. She's with me a block away. It started in the storage shed. Fire crew is here, but I thought it best to call you."

"I'm on my way." He shoved the phone in his pocket then turned back to Eric and Brooke. "There's a fire at Lainey's. I'm heading over there. Let the family know."

"Hey, do you need help?" Eric called as Cam dashed through the door to his truck.

"No. I'll call if I need anything."

******

It took Cam almost thirty minutes to get to town, wind his way through the crowd gathered on surrounding streets, and make his way to the police barricade.

"Buck Towers called me. I need to find him."

The young officer pointed toward a car near Lainey's house.

Cam sprinted down the street, glancing to his side to watch as the crew started their cleanup efforts. It appeared the fire had been contained to the storage shed and one side of the old garage near the back of Lainey's property.

Lainey saw him approach and started forward. "I'm sorry to drag you back out here..."

Cam pulled her into him, ignoring her apology, relief flooding through his body as he realized she wasn't hurt. She wrapped her arms around Cam and buried her head in his shoulder.

"Looks like the shed is the only casualty. Don't know how it didn't jump to the house." Buck stood next to Cam, arms folded as he surveyed the damage. "They do know it was arson. Apparently whoever did this made no attempt to make it look like an accident. The fire chief said it appears the arsonist poured gasoline around the shed and back fence. This fire isn't a coincidence, Ms. Devlin."

"Not around the garage?" Cam asked.

"That's the strange part. They'll be back tomorrow to check further, but for now, it looks like only the fence and shed were targeted."

Buck's words confirmed what Lainey had already guessed. Lainey pulled back from Cam. "I guess I'd better check it out."

"I'm coming with you."

They walked around the property, keeping out of the way as the cleanup crew finished their work and loaded equipment into their waiting trucks. The heat from the embers could be felt yards away, soot still drifting in flakes to the ground as smoke clung to the air. They stood several feet away, scanning the area for anything salvageable. Cam could see the remains of Lainey's bicycle in the rubble. Other than that, everything was a mass of twisted metal and ash.

"Get your things. You're staying with me tonight."

"No. I'm staying here. The house will be destroyed if he comes back and no one is home." She started toward the house, determined not to let the arsonist drive her away.

Cam gripped her arm, spinning her to face him. "Listen to me, Lainey. You can't stay here. The person doing this can't be in their right mind, which means no one can guess what he'll do next. Buck is sending cars around every fifteen minutes, plus your neighbors will be on alert. Don't be obstinate. Your life is worth more than this house." His gaze held hers, a sense of urgency and fear flickering between them.

"I'm not trying to be obstinate." A sigh escaped her lips, her chest heaving at the reality of what she faced. She ran shaky fingers through her hair then took a deep breath.

"You don't have to stay with me, but you need to get away from here. Is there anyone else you can call?" Although his words were calm, reassuring, he didn't want Lainey staying with anyone except him.

"There's just Mark and he's still in Idaho."

"My place it is. Get what you need for a few days." He held up his hand when she started to protest. "Just in case you need to stay longer." *Or want to stay longer,* Cam thought as he followed her inside the house.

******

He peered around the corner from his hiding place. No one had noticed him wander toward the street along with the other neighbors who watched the fire. Lainey had dashed right past him, unaware he'd been the one to start the blaze. It had been easy. Most people in the neighborhood worked during the day, making it possible for him to approach from the alley in broad daylight, pour some gasoline around the shed, strike a match, and disappear within minutes.

She'd walked up to the policeman who stood by his car a few yards from her house. It seemed obvious from her posture and gestures that the fire rattled her just as he'd hoped. Good, perhaps now she'd understand the threats were serious.

He watched as she and the guy from the night before disappeared inside then returned a few minutes later with a small duffle bag and computer case. She was leaving.

The arsonist let out a breath. He didn't want to harm her, or anyone else, even though he would if needed. No, he'd target others until she got the message that Fire Mountain wasn't safe any longer.

******

"The guest room is down the hall on the right. My room is on the left. We share a bath, but it's a good size— almost as large as my bedroom." Cam tossed the bag of takeout on the counter and made coffee while he spoke. Lainey hadn't eaten since lunch, and even though she had no interest in food, he knew the effects of the fire would wear off and she'd be famished.

"Nice place. Have you lived in it long?" Lainey had changed into jeans and a snug fitting t-shirt. He watched her stroll around the room, looking at the few pictures he'd hung and photos of his family.

"Since I arrived from San Francisco. Heath built several of these cabins within a couple miles of the main house. Eric stays in one of them." He glanced at the compact kitchen that opened into the dining and living rooms. "I like it. Besides, it comes with my job, which is a heck of a deal compared to the rent I paid in California."

She looked up, a vague smile curving her lips. "The family rate?"

"Perhaps. I'll tell you, though, Heath doesn't make allowances for any of the family members, including Jace, who is his brother, part owner, and senior vice president. I've no doubt he wouldn't hesitate to call us out if we didn't produce."

Lainey eyed the bag of takeout and felt her stomach rumble.

"Sounds like you might be a little hungry," Cam smiled before grabbing a plate and silverware. "Here you go. Dig in."

They sat across from each other at the small table, Lainey doing her best to finish an oversized burrito with salsa while Cam sipped his coffee.

Lainey crumpled her napkin and threw on the plate. "Thanks."

"For what?"

"Being there tonight, letting me stay here, the food," she eyed her empty plate then took a long swallow of water.

"You must be exhausted after everything that's happened." Cam pushed from his chair, picked up her plate, and carried it to the sink. "What about tomorrow at the preschool? Do you need to go in?"

"I don't have a choice. The parents depend on me and I have just two helpers this week. The third one is visiting relatives in Texas for a few more days. I'll see if there's a chance I can get away around lunchtime and have someone else close up. I need to meet the insurance adjuster at the house sometime tomorrow, plus an arson investigator is supposed to call. Sergeant Towers said they usually come up from the valley."

Cam handed her coffee with cream and some sugar, the way he'd seen her make it at the coffee house he'd taken her to weeks before. It seemed like a lifetime since that night, their kiss, and his decision to call it off with Megan. So much had happened yet he and Lainey were still treading lightly, afraid to push their tentative friendship too far.

"I may need to find a substitute for a few days. Don't know how easy it will be to find someone."

Cam's eyes shot to hers. "I have an idea." He grabbed his phone. "Hi Caroline, it's Cam. You wouldn't want to pinch hit at a preschool for a few days, would you?" A few minutes later he set the phone back on the kitchen counter. That's when he noticed Lainey's stupefied expression.

"And that was...?"

"My aunt, Caroline MacLaren. She used to teach preschool before she and Jace got married. She's mentioned a few times how routine her life has become, and I thought this could work out for both of you."

"You sure she's fine with it?"

"More than that. She sounded excited. She'll meet you at the school tomorrow morning at six-thirty."

Lainey stared at him, confused by why he kept helping her, yet not knowing what she would have done without him.

"It seems like lately I'm always thanking you," she murmured as she rinsed out her coffee cup then placed her hands on the counter, her eyes riveted on his. "I don't understand. Why are you helping me?"

He'd hoped she wouldn't question his motives, dig too deep into why he couldn't let her walk through her troubles alone.

He shrugged his shoulders. "You're my SAR partner, at least until you get settled in."

Her eyes never wavered from his. "And you'd do this for any partner?"

"Possibly. Probably."

"I see." She'd hoped for a different answer, one that would let her know she mattered to him as more than a partner or acquaintance. No matter what she'd told herself the last few weeks, she wanted Cam and hoped at some point he might want to see if anything between them could work.

Lainey checked the time. "It's pretty late. Guess I'll turn in." She started for the hall, then called over her shoulder. "Thanks again, Cam. You've been great."

Well, damn, Cam thought as she disappeared down the hall. He had hoped she'd relax, keep him company for a while, and show an interest in rebuilding what they'd lost when he'd failed to tell her about Megan. At least she had agreed to stay, and that in itself said something.

Cam turned off the lights and headed to bed. He'd just closed his bedroom door when he heard the shower start up. Images of Lainey, stripping out of her jeans and t-shirt, stepping under the warm spray, and letting the water sluice over her body assailed Cam. He groaned as his body tightened at the vision his mind formed. What he should do was get undressed, slide into bed, and get a good night's sleep. What he wanted was something different.

He stripped down to nothing except his boxers and lay across his bed, an arm resting over his eyes, and tried without success to rid his mind of Lainey and her activities across the hall. It couldn't be healthy, the kind of pull she had over him, almost as if she was sucking him into a place from where he'd never return. Yet the more she was near, the less resistance he felt, and the more he wanted to be drawn into her life, and not as just a friend.

He heard the shower stop and a few minutes later heard the bathroom door open and close. His turn. Cam glanced down the hall. She'd disappeared into her room. He stepped into the bathroom and walked toward the shower to turn on the faucet. He'd just reached for the light when Lainey walked in, wearing nothing except a bath towel which wrapped around her body and tucked in at the front.

She gasped and stepped backwards, knocking into the door frame, and almost unhinging the towel that had loosened from the rapid movement. "I'm sorry...I didn't see you..." Her gaze locked on his. She could feel her face redden and dropped her eyes to his muscled chest, sprinkled with crisp, blond hair. Her heart pounded erratically as an image of the two of them together took hold. She turned toward her room, then felt Cam's gentle grip on her shoulder stopping her retreat.

He didn't say a word, simply turned her toward him, and let his gaze wander from her face, down her still damp arms and legs, to her toes, which were painted with soft pink polish. He lifted a hand to stroke his knuckles down her cheek to her jaw, then ran a finger along the soft column of her neck.

Lainey stood motionless, knowing she should return to the shelter and safety of her bedroom. Her obstinate legs wouldn't obey. They stayed rooted in place as her body reacted to his touch. She gazed up into warm brown eyes that had turned a deep chocolate. She moistened her dry lips, unaware of the effect the small action had on Cam. He let his hand move around to the back of her neck, drawing her toward him, lowering his head until their lips were a breath apart.

Cam searched her eyes then lowered his mouth to hers, running his warm lips over hers before pulling her tight and taking what he'd wanted for weeks.

Lainey's body heated, warm currents flowing from her toes to her face. She grasped his arms, her heart hammering as her body arched into his.

Cam's urgency slowed and his hands moved over her damp shoulders, down her body to rest on her towel-covered hips. He pulled her close, never breaking the contact of his lips on hers, and let her feel how she affected him.

She wrapped her arms around his neck, a soft sigh escaping at his gentle yet firm touch.

"Cam," she breathed out when he pulled back to look into her passion-filled eyes. The want and need she saw scared and excited her. She lifted her hand between them, tugged gently on the small knot, and let the towel drift to the floor.

Cam's mouth went dry. She was the most beautiful woman he'd ever seen and he wanted her with a desperation he'd never felt before.

"I want you, Cam." Her soft words penetrated his senses and in one, smooth motion, she was in his arms. His mouth found hers as he carried her across the hall and into his bedroom, closing the door behind them.

Chapter Fifteen

Lainey felt warm fingers run down her back and startled at the touch. They'd made love over and over until each gave into their body's need for sleep.

Cam placed soft kisses on her neck and down her shoulders, sending shivers through her body, and causing heat to once again flash through her body. She should have been spent from their long night. Her thoughts drifted for a brief moment to her house and the fire, before Cam's kisses caused her to lose all coherent thought. She gave in to his continued caresses, and on a sigh, turned into his arms.

An hour later Cam followed her to the preschool. She'd be a little late, but in Lainey's mind, it was worth it. They'd lingered in bed, talking, trying to make sense of what each felt, and finally deciding to take it a day at a time. Neither regretted their night together and neither wanted to walk away.

Lainey had called her neighbor, Pete, before leaving Cam's house. Pete sounded like he hadn't slept all night, and he probably hadn't. He'd watched the street from his large picture window and checked outside several times until dawn. Everything had remained quiet.

Caroline waved when she saw Cam's truck pull into the lot behind a red SUV, which she figured to be Lainey's.

"You must be Caroline," Lainey called as she jumped out of her car. "I'm Lainey Devlin. Sorry to keep you waiting."

"No problem at all." Caroline turned as Cam walked up beside her and gave her a quick kiss on the cheek.

"Thanks, Caroline. It's great of you to jump into this without notice."

Caroline laughed. "Are you kidding? Life around Jace and Heath is always unpredictable, so I've become an expert at spontaneity. Well, let's get started."

******

Lainey met the insurance adjuster a couple of hours later. The back area of the property looked worse in the daylight, with charred wood, ash everywhere, and debris that hadn't been destroyed yet no longer held a useful purpose.

"Any idea of the value of the shed's contents?" The female adjuster asked as she snapped a few more pictures.

"The bicycle cost six hundred dollars new about two years ago. The tools and most everything else in the shed couldn't have been worth much, maybe two or three hundred dollars at most."

"Have you gotten an estimate on rebuilding the shed and fence, and replacing the siding on your garage?"

"No. The fire just happened last night. How soon do you need it?"

"Within a few days. It's up to you. The sooner I have all the information, the sooner we can release the funds so you can start rebuilding." She snapped her notebook shut and handed Lainey her card. "Call me when you get the estimate."

Lainey pulled out her phone.

"Cam Sinclair." The sound of his voice caused butterflies to form in the pit of her stomach.

"Hi, Cam. It's me, Lainey."

Cam sat back in his chair, a broad smile breaking out across his face. "Hi. How'd it go with the adjuster?"

"Okay, I guess. I need an estimate to replace the shed and fence, plus the siding on the garage. I didn't realize it had been scorched until I saw it this morning."

"No problem. I'll contact our contractor, Seth Garner. He can probably have someone out by this afternoon."

"That would be great."

"What are you doing for lunch?"

"No plans. I guess it depends on what time the contractor can come out."

"Drive out toward my office. There's a great lunch place about four miles from your house." He gave her the address. "Noon work for you?"

"That's fine, unless the contractor calls and needs to stop by then."

"I'm sure he'll work around it. See you at noon." Cam clicked off, leaving Lainey to wait for the call from the contractor, and looked forward to lunch.

It amazed Lainey how things had changed in the last twenty-four hours. Nothing about yesterday or last night could have been anticipated when she got out of bed before sunrise. Just one day later, everything was different.

Cam called Seth, confirming that the estimator would set an appointment for after two o'clock.

He looked up as his office door opened and Eric poked his head in.

"Do you have a minute, Cam?" Eric asked then disappeared back into the hallway.

Cam followed Eric to Heath's office where Jace MacLaren, Doug Hester, the company's CFO, and Colt Minton, the company attorney, stood near the window, conferring quietly while Heath finished a phone call. He hung up and motioned everyone to the conference table and wasted no time getting to the point of their meeting.

"Based on Cam's site visit and input from Jace, Doug, and Colt, I've made the decision to go forward with the purchase of Damon's business. Cam, you'll take the lead on integration. Let me know who else you need and it'll be handled. You'll need to be out there next week. Don't plan to stay over on weekends. You'll fly out Monday mornings and fly back Friday afternoons for the next few weeks. We'll revisit everything when you feel it's necessary."

Heath shuffled through a couple of papers before pulling out the one he sought.

"Now to new business. We're looking at buying a business in Montana that provides bulls to the rodeo circuit. There are three partners, two want to sell, the third doesn't. The two contacted me confidentially, asking to meet and discuss a potential sale. This is tricky as all three have been close friends for years and own equal shares in the company." Heath glanced at Jace, then continued. "The two want to retire, or at least cut back their responsibilities to focus on their families. We'll address those issues if we believe the acquisition would be a fit for us. Eric, you'll be part of the evaluation team along with Colt and Doug. Cam will fly up to help evaluate after we've made a preliminary decision to proceed. Jace and I will stay out of it until we have more information from the three of you. I've told them we wouldn't be able to start evaluations for at least four months, which is agreeable to the two partners."

Eric nodded as he jotted down notes. "Have you met the third partner?"

Jace and Heath shared a look before Heath spoke up. "He's our brother. Rafe."

******

"Wow, I didn't suspect the Montana business had anything to do with Rafe." Eric and Cam walked back to their offices, discussing the bomb Heath had dropped on them.

"Trey and I talked about Rafe a little when I visited him last year at the base. That's all I know about him besides what we've been told about the brothers having a falling out before Trey was born. Rafe moved around, finally settling in Montana. Guess none of them have seen each other since."

"That's a long time to hold a grudge." Eric stopped at his office. "Guess this one's going to be a real learning experience—for both of us."

"It sure is." Cam checked his watch. "I'm off to a lunch appointment."

"That so?" Eric could guess who his brother planned to meet. "Say hi to Lainey for me," he grinned before closing his office door.

Cam pulled into the restaurant a couple of minutes late, noticing right away that Lainey's car wasn't in the lot. Good, he'd have time to get a table and make a couple of quick calls. Fifteen minutes passed with no sign of Lainey. He punched in her number and left a voice message. Cam waited another fifteen minutes before paying for his drink and driving toward her house. Something was wrong. Lainey would've called him if she couldn't make their lunch date.

He pulled into her drive to see the SUV parked near the back of the driveway. Cam bounded up the front steps, knocked, and looked through the newly replaced window while he waited. Her purse sat on the dining room table and a jacket had been thrown across a chair. He knocked again, called her name, and waited, thinking she may be upstairs or in the laundry room. Still no answer or sign of Lainey.

Cam ran around to the side. Both the kitchen and laundry room doors were locked. He looked around the yard. That's when he spotted her phone on the ground near the burned rubble of the old shed. He grabbed it. The last two calls were from him while he'd waited for her at the restaurant. Cam didn't waste any more time.

"Is Sergeant Towers available?" Cam's heart raced as he processed the possibilities of what had happened at Lainey's since they'd last spoken. All of them left a sick feeling in his gut.

"Towers."

"Buck, it's Cam Sinclair. Lainey, Ms. Devlin, is gone. She was supposed to meet me for lunch. When she didn't show up I drove to her house. No one's here but her purse is inside and her phone was on the ground in the back. Something's not right."

"I'm on my way."

The police headquarters were no more than five minutes from Lainey's house, and that's how long it took before Cam heard the sirens. Buck had wasted no time getting on the road. A minute later two squad cars pulled up front, two officers getting out of each one and approaching Cam.

"Show me what you've seen," Buck called as he and Cam ran toward the front porch.

Cam didn't have a key, but that didn't stop Buck from getting inside. Nothing felt right about the scene in front of them. A full cup of coffee, now cold, sat on the kitchen counter. A small television in the living room displayed an afternoon news program. A notebook with a list of items in the shed lay next to Lainey's purse on the dining room table—the name and phone number of the insurance adjuster written at the top.

"Sergeant? There's a neighbor outside who'd like to speak with you," one of the other officers called from the front door.

"What can I do for you, Mr..."

"I'm Pete Gomez. I live next door." He pointed to the house on the side of Lainey's house closest to her driveway. "I just got home and saw the cars. Is this about Lainey?"

"It is. Did your wife see anything today?"

"She told me an old brown van had been parked in the alley for at least an hour this morning—got there sometime before eleven. Maia, my wife, kept checking on it but never saw anyone inside. Anyway, she'd gone to the front yard and saw Lainey come out the kitchen door. Not long after, Maia heard an engine start up in the alley. She checked the back, and sure enough, the van was gone. She didn't see Lainey again and was about to call you folks when he pulled up." Pete acknowledged Cam with a nod of his head.

"I'd like to speak to your wife, Mr. Gomez."

"Sure. She's out front."

Buck followed Pete outside, Cam close behind, when Cam's phone rang. The SAR headquarters number appeared.

"Cam, we have a situation." Frank's voice sounded calm yet urgent. "A man called. He's stranded on some type of rock cliff near Platt Mountain. Says somebody pushed him off the trail then left. Mentioned we can find him if we locate his brown van. God only knows how the guy got cell service up there."

Cam's eyes grew wide. "A brown van?"

"Yeah. Guess the guy drove up there. After that I don't know any specifics except someone he met pushed him off the edge of the trail. The guy landed on a rock outcropping."

"Frank. Listen to me. Lainey is missing." Cam could hear Frank cursing through the phone. "I'm at her house with Buck Towers. The neighbor said a brown van was seen in her alley not long before she disappeared. Did he mention anything about a woman?"

"No. You think he's connected to this?"

"I don't know. I'll grab Buck. Who else do you have available?"

"My brother Tony and a couple of others."

"I'll be there in ten minutes. I need everything you have about the man's location." Cam shoved the phone into this pocket.

"Buck! There's a stranded hiker near Pratt Mountain. He says someone pushed him off the trail and he landed on a rock shelf. He told Frank we'll find him if we locate his brown van." Cam ran toward his truck, then called back to Buck. "You coming?"

Chapter Sixteen

"There it is." Tony pointed to a brown van parked to the side of an old county access road. "It can't be more than twenty feet away from the edge."

Cam pulled to a stop and jumped out, Tony and Buck following as Cam ran out onto a small trail toward a drop-off. A second truck stopped, and four more men emerged—two SAR members and two police officers.

"Hello! Anyone down there?" Cam cupped his hands and shouted.

"Here! I'm down here!"

Cam and Tony peeked over the edge enough to see a man about twenty feet down the side of the mountain, crouched low on a shelf that appeared to be about six feet in diameter.

Cam started to grab his gear before Tony put a hand on his shoulder.

"We'll handle this one, Cam," motioning toward the other volunteers. "You stay up here with Buck."

"But..."

"You need to be up here when we bring the guy up. You understand?"

Cam hesitated before accepting that Tony's approach made sense. He'd be at the top with Buck, able to hear his story, and perhaps locate Lainey.

"Sir, you've got to see this." The youngest of the deputies spoke to Buck, indicating the van the other officers had been searching.

Cam followed Buck to the van, curious as to what the men had found.

"Shit," Buck murmured when he looked inside. Several coiled ropes, chain cutters, duct tape, cans of gasoline, a bag of rags, a crow bar, a case of water, a laptop and other electronic gear, a leather case holding four knives, a couple of blankets and two pillows, extra clothes, and several pairs of shoes. "This is quite a setup. Whatever the man does, he's organized about it." Buck turned toward the deputy. "I want lots of pictures and a detailed list of the contents."

Cam's eyes continued to scan the inside of the van, locking on one piece of paper on the side, near the middle. "What's that?"

The deputy climbed inside, careful not to disturb anything, and snatched up what appeared to be a card. "It says Sunshine Preschool." He crawled out and handed the card to Buck.

"That's Lainey's business." Cam ran back to the edge of the cliff as the man's head appeared over the rim. Five minutes later the gear had been removed from around the man, he'd been placed in handcuffs, and sat rigid, on the ground with his back against a boulder.

Buck pulled out his notepad and got right to business. "What's your name?"

"Hey, I didn't do anything. This guy pushed me off the edge and took off."

Cam stood two feet away, impatient, angry, and ready to beat the truth out of the guy.

"Your name." Buck's voice held an edge Cam hadn't heard before.

"Benny."

"Last name?"

"Kurtz."

"All right, Mr. Kurtz, is that your van back on the road?"

"Why?"

Buck got into Benny's face. "Is that your van?"

"Yeah, it's mine."

Buck pulled out Lainey's card. "Who does this belong to?"

Benny took a quick look then turned away. "Don't know. Never seen it before."

"It was found in your van. It belongs to a woman who was taken from her home a few hours ago. Neighbors saw your van, can identify it, and identify you. You're in a heap of trouble. It will go better for you if you tell us where the woman is."

Benny pursed his lips, refusing to speak.

"All right then. Deputy, book this man on arson, kidnapping, and possible murder charges..."

Cam's gut clenched at Buck's words.

"Wait..."

"You have something to say, Mr. Kurtz?"

"He took her. Pushed me off the path and took her."

"Who took her and where did they go?"

"The guy who hired me to scare the Devlin woman. Don't know for sure where he took her."

"Scare her or kill her?"

Benny jolted at the accusation. "I wouldn't have killed her. He just wanted me to scare her, get her to leave town, move back with him. She didn't scare much, so he wanted me to grab her, bring her up here to him so they could talk, in private."

"That why he pushed you off the cliff?"

Benny looked down into his lap. "He didn't push me. The woman ran. When he caught her, she shoved him, and he fell toward me. I lost my footing and slipped."

Buck and Cam exchanged looks, not sure what version of Benny's story to believe. For now, what they needed was the man's name and description.

"His name, Benny. I need the name."

"Don't know his first name, but last name is Crafton."

"Shit," Cam spit out and lunged toward Benny before the deputies pulled him back.

"You know him, Cam?"

"Crafton is the last name of Lainey's ex-fiancé. Robert Crafton."

"That's him." Benny fidgeted on the hard ground. "That's the name she called him. Robert."

******

172

Cam ran to his truck, pulled out his phone, and started making calls as soon as Buck had given him the description of Crafton and the make, model, and color of the car Crafton drove. The deputies loaded Benny into one of the trucks while Buck placed emergency calls to law enforcement agencies about the kidnapping.

"Eric, it's Cam. Lainey's been taken by her ex-fiancé, Robert Crafton. I'm with Buck Towers on Pratt Mountain." Cam paused a moment. "I don't know what the family can do. Right now, just be aware that I'm okay and I'll do what I can to find Lainey."

"Hold on, Cam."

Cam could hear voices in the background before his stepfather came on the line.

"Cam, it's Heath. How can we help?"

"Don't know just yet. Buck's calling it out to all the agencies. He says the FBI may get involved if Crafton crosses the state line. Personally, I think the man would be insane to try and take her back to Idaho. I think he'll stay in Arizona, try to talk Lainey into moving back to Idaho and marrying him."

"Give me the details and I'll put our people on alert. You can stay with Buck or come back here and take the helicopter. Let me know and I'll have it ready for you."

"I'll be there in thirty minutes." Cam jumped into the cab of his truck as Buck climbed in next to him and Tony slid into the back. "Heath's getting the helicopter ready for me. I'll take Eric and Todd, the other pilot. You can reach me through Heath."

"Cam, it's best if you let us handle the search for Crafton. Who knows what the man will do. You're not trained in this, we are." Buck didn't hide his displeasure at Cam's desire to hunt down Crafton, but as a husband, he understood how the young man felt.

"I'll just be using the helicopter to help. Maybe we'll spot something from the air."

Cam sped down the rutted mountain road, wasting no time getting to the airfield and up into the sky where he might spot Crafton. His gut told him the man wouldn't hurt Lainey. Crafton's goal was to talk her into leaving Fire Mountain, something the man wanted with a desperation that had driven him to actions most would consider delusional.

"Roger that, Buck." Todd turned toward Cam as he ascended and turned the helicopter north toward the Arizona-California border. "We're okay to go with our plan. They'll cover the east and south."

Cam, Eric, and Todd all guessed Crafton would head west, then north, staying south of the Nevada border and west of Flagstaff. There were several small towns in that direction, any one of which would be the perfect place to hide as those communities relied on a small number of officers for a vast area of the state.

Eric sat in the back, binoculars up as he scanned the ground below. They kept to the major roads most the time, occasionally veering off to circle specific areas before heading back to their pre-set route.

"Could he have picked a more common car as a rental?" Eric grumbled. "A white, four-door import. There must be thousands of those between Fire Mountain and Nevada."

"Kurtz said it had Idaho plates. That's a misstep. He should've rented a car here, then switched in Nevada, and again in Utah." Todd peered out the front and side windows, having the same issues as Eric—too many cars that looked alike.

"Problem is, he'd have to use different credit cards and ID each time. Plus it would hold up his progress." Eric slid to the other side of the helicopter and looked down. "That's assuming he talks Lainey into going back with him, which I doubt. She seems to be the type of woman who'd dig in her heels at being ordered around. Somehow, I don't think our Cam's preschool teacher is going to cross the state line."

Cam listened to the banter and hoped Eric was right. He knew for a fact she could be stubborn and independent. Now she had to stay calm and believe they'd find her before anyone got hurt.

******

"Why are you doing this, Robert? You know I won't change my mind and return to Bluebird Falls. My life is in Fire Mountain, not Idaho." She tried to keep him talking, distracted, and off-guard. She found he slowed his speed when they spoke, especially if he became agitated. The two lane road they'd been on for almost two hours would hit a major intersection twenty miles north.

"You're confused Lainey. I don't know what happened a few months ago to make you change your mind and break off our engagement, but I'm certain in time, you'll realize you made a mistake and want to come back. I'm simply speeding up the time table."

He hadn't tied her hands, locked the door, or threatened her in any way. She truly believed Robert thought hiring Kurtz to scare and intimidate her had been an appropriate way to drive her back to Idaho, and him. She shook her head when she realized how irrational he'd become. Or perhaps he'd always been this way and she'd just never figured it out.

"Robert, if you turn around now and take me back, I won't press charges. I'll do whatever I can to see you get back home and continue to practice law. You do know what you're doing is kidnapping, right?"

"Of course, I know most people would consider this kidnapping, but I don't. I'm taking you on a drive until you're convinced I'm the man you're supposed to be with, not some wealthy businessman from Arizona."

Lainey's heart raced at the reference to Cam. Robert hadn't mentioned anything about him until now. "I don't know what you mean."

He cast her a disdainful look. "Don't play dumb, Lainey, it doesn't become you. Sinclair, the man you've been seeing, and sleeping with. Ah, you thought I didn't know? Well I do, and regardless, I'm willing to take you back and rebuild what you threw away."

He knew about Cam and yet he thought she'd just leave her life behind, return to something that meant nothing to her anymore, and act like none of the past weeks had occurred. The thought that Robert might actually be crazy scared her more than any of the previous threats. She knew from her SAR experience that desperate people took risks that put them and others in danger. Their goal became more important than the risk.

Lainey closed her eyes and tried to relax. There would be an opportunity to get away from Robert. She just needed to be patient, let him make a mistake, and run.

******

"Cam, do you see that car just ahead? The white, four door with red, white, and blue Idaho plates?" Eric leaned as far forward as possible, trying to make out the passengers. "It's hard to tell from here but it looks like there's a man driving. I believe a woman's in the passenger seat. I can't see anyone else."

"Todd, contact Buck. Tell him we may have spotted Crafton. Have him get people to the freeway intersection a few miles ahead and block all entrances. He'll have just ten or fifteen minutes before the car gets onto the interstate."

Todd wasted no time getting Buck on the radio. "Done. He's got cars on the way and another helicopter.

Even if Crafton makes it onto the freeway, he'll have nowhere to go. He'll be trapped."

Cam slowed the helicopter to keep pace with the car that had pulled a half mile ahead of them. He didn't want to alert Crafton to their presence, and at the same time couldn't afford to lose him.

******

"Do you hear that?" Crafton shifted in his seat to look around.

"Hear what?"

"Sounds like a helicopter. Maybe behind us. Take a look." Robert kept his eyes on the road, not changing speed or acting as if anyone might be chasing them. Worse, he had convinced himself that Lainey still wanted to be with him and return to Bluebird Falls.

She looked behind her and up to see a helicopter following about a mile away. She'd heard it for some time, yet hadn't let on, hoping it would be someone trying to locate her. Enough time had passed that Cam would know something had happened, and in her heart, she knew he wouldn't stop until he found her.

"Do you see anything?"

"There's a helicopter quite a ways back. I can't tell what it's doing from here. Do you want to slow down so I can get a better look?"

"No. We're almost to the freeway. We'll get something to eat, find a place to stay the night, and talk. There's much I have to tell you."

Lainey realized Robert had set himself up in a delusional world of his own making, believing what he wanted, and trusting others believed the same. He didn't comprehend that soon he'd be in jail and she'd be on her way to Fire Mountain, and Cam.

******

"Roger that, Buck. Thanks." Todd turned to Cam. "Everyone's in place. There were roadblocks at the freeway entrances already and now there are a few more officers. It won't be long now."

Cam scanned the horizon, searching for a place to set down. He could see the freeway up ahead and began a slow descent.

"You see that?" Eric asked, pointing toward the interstate. "They're out in force."

"Crafton will see them soon. We'll follow if he makes a move to turn around. If he doesn't, I'll find a place to set down." Cam stayed focused on the path ahead, his intention to hover over the car while looking for a suitable landing spot near the freeway intersection.

"Looks like Crafton spotted them. He's braking." Eric continued to watch through the binoculars.

Lainey saw the patrol cars, lights flashing, at the same time as Robert. In his current state, she had no idea what Robert would do—try to drive around them, turn back, or give himself up. At one point in her life, Lainey had thought she knew the man, what drove him, and how he'd react when angry. She felt differently now.

"What will you do, Robert?"

"Stop and talk to them. Find out what the commotion's about." His calm voice disturbed her more than if he'd panicked and tried to run.

Lainey decided to sit tight. She'd be ready to jump if he stopped the car. She had no intention of being around when he discussed her abduction and tried to talk his way out of what had turned into an extremely serious situation. One that Lainey was sure Robert didn't grasp. She placed her hand on the door handle as Robert pulled to a stop, turned off the engine, and cast a look at Lainey.

"You stay here. I'll explain you've decided to go back to Idaho with me. This shouldn't take long."

He opened his door and climbed out to shouts from the officers who stood no more than fifteen feet away, partially hidden behind their cruisers, with guns drawn.

"Stop where you are! Put your hands in the air!"

Lainey didn't hesitate. Before Robert took two steps from his car, she dashed out the other side and ran toward a highway patrol car off to her right, the farthest point of rescue from Robert.

"I'm Lainey Devlin," she choked out as she approached an officer who grabbed her arm and yanked her down beside him.

"Stay down, Ms. Devlin. Did he hurt you?" The officer couldn't have been more than twenty-five, yet he had the air of someone with years of experience.

"No, I'm fine." Lainey took a deep breath, attempting to rein in the fear she'd felt the last few hours. "He's delusional. Robert believes I wanted to leave with him."

The officer glanced down at her, but only nodded.

Lainey's head swiveled at the whirling sound of the helicopter as it prepared to land about a hundred yards from her on a vast, open field. She watched as it landed, the engine shut down, and the pilot jumped out. Cam.

"Cam!" She started to rise, run toward him, when the officer pulled her back down.

"Stay here. Let him come to you." He never took his eyes off the scene in front of them. Robert Crafton continued to rant about something while an officer cuffed him and assisted him into the back of a patrol car. The officer let loose of his hold on Lainey once Crafton was secured and no longer a threat. "All right. Go ahead."

Lainey wasted no time. She dashed toward Cam, who had come within a few yards, and threw herself at him, wrapping her arms around his neck, and holding on tight.

"Cam, you came for me."

He held her to him, relief flooding his body, and thanking God they'd found her.

"Did you think I wouldn't? I love you, Lainey," he whispered in her ear before pulling back enough to cover her mouth with his in a hard, possessive kiss.

Eric and Todd stood just feet away, smiling, and relieved they'd found Lainey before Crafton did something that couldn't be undone.

Cam ended the kiss and held her at arm's length while his gaze roamed from her head to her feet. "Are you hurt?"

"No, Robert didn't hurt me. He never tied my hands or secured me at all. The whole situation had been too incredible." She turned toward the police car where Robert sat, still trying to reason with the officer who sat in the driver's seat, and nodding toward Lainey, as if she would explain everything. She'd be happy to explain, although she knew Robert wouldn't like what she had to say.

Cam wrapped an arm around her shoulders and pulled her tight.

"Looks like he won't bother you any longer, sweetheart."

She gazed up at him, her face breaking into a tentative smile. She started to say something, then stopped.

"What is it?" Cam asked.

"Nothing, except I'm glad it's over and you're here."

He turned her to face him. "I'll always be here for you, Lainey. Always."

Epilogue

Four months later…

Cam supported himself on one arm and gazed down at Lainey as she slept. He never tired at the sight of her, especially in the mornings after a passion-filled night of making love. She'd decided to let her black hair grow back to its longer length, and he reached down to capture strands of hair and sweep them off her face. He bent to place a soft kiss on her forehead, and watched her stir.

She turned her head toward him as her eyes opened a crack. "What time is it?"

"After seven, Mrs. Sinclair."

Her eyes opened and locked on his, crinkling at the corners, as a smile pierced her face. "I do like the sound of that." Her sleepy voice indicated how exhausted she felt. They'd married several weeks before and each day still felt like a honeymoon.

Cam stroked a finger down her cheek and followed it with feathery kisses until he claimed her mouth with his. She wrapped her arms around his neck, and pulled him to her, letting her fingers run through his hair.

"When do you fly back?" she whispered against his lips, then drew back.

"Ten o'clock. We have time," Cam answered as he lowered his mouth again.

"You do. I have a meeting at eight at the preschool." She placed one more kiss on his lips before rolling from the bed and heading toward the shower. "The new assistant manager is taking over as of today and I want to be there."

She and Cam had discussed at length her desire to continue her preschool after the news of his promotion to president of their new acquisition in Cold Creek, Colorado. The previous president retired after an unexpected heart attack. Heath hadn't wasted a minute putting Cam in charge. Cam's new duties required him to be in Colorado each week from Monday morning until Friday afternoon. The company jet, which he co-piloted, shuttled him back and forth.

However, neither he nor Lainey wanted to be apart for days at a time indefinitely. So, they'd compromised. She hired an assistant manager to help with the day-to-day operations of her preschool, which freed Lainey to travel to Cold Creek with Cam most weeks. This was the woman's second week and already Lainey felt she'd hired the perfect person.

"Next week, you'll fly with me to Cold Creek. Our house will be ready to move into by Tuesday, but believe me, there's still a lot to do." He stepped into the shower behind her, soaped a soft cloth, and began to run it over her sleek body.

"That's all right. I'd much rather keep busy than sit around the house waiting for you to get home." She finished rinsing her hair and turned toward him, her eyes sweeping down his magnificent body.

"By the way, I have an offer for you."

She glanced up at him. "What kind of offer?"

"Heath and I have been discussing the need for a preschool near the facility in Cold Creek. There isn't one for miles, yet the area is surrounded by new neighborhoods and young families. Most drive into town to drop off their children, then turn around to head back to our area for work. They do the round trip again after work. Even if you don't want to run it, we could use your help finding a location and setting it up. What do you think?"

Her eyes lit up and Cam knew he had her. "I like the idea. Can it wait until we get settled, maybe in a month?"

His reply was cut off by the ringing of her phone. She grabbed a towel and stepped out of the shower, picking up the phone on the counter.

"This is Lainey." She fell silent as the caller talked for several minutes. "I see. I don't believe that will work, but I'm happy to recommend someone. Okay, fine. That's great news. Thanks so much for calling."

"Good news?" Cam stood beside her, hair damp, a towel wrapped around his waist.

"Robert's been sentenced to time in a mental facility. His evaluation came back with a diagnosis of strong delusional tendencies accompanied by some form of schizophrenia." She placed the phone down and turned back to Cam. "Such a waste."

He wrapped his arms around her, pulling her close. "At least he'll get the treatment he needs. He may never be able to practice law again, which is no doubt for the best."

"He asked that I come to Bluebird Falls to take care of selling his house."

"No." Cam's firm response and set features confirmed what Lainey already thought.

"That's what I told them." She finished dressing before heading to the kitchen for coffee, handing Cam a cup when he joined her. Lainey glanced at her watch.

"Guess I'd better get going." She reached up and placed a kiss on his cheek. "Call me tonight?"

"Definitely," Cam replied as his phone rang. He shook his head then reached into his pocket to check the caller ID—his sister, Brooke. "Hey, Brooke. What's up?" His face sobered as he listened. "I'm on my way now. No, Brooke, I won't wait to find out what's happening, I'm getting on a plane within the hour—period. Now, let me speak to one of your new friends."

Cam listened, jotting down names and numbers before asking to speak with Brooke again.

Lainey watched, concern crossing her face as she watched her husband deal with the news from Brooke.

"I'll call as soon as I land. Yes, I'll explain it to everyone, and take special care about what I say to Mom. You do understand she'll call you back as soon as she hears the news and will want to fly out, right?"

What can I do? Lainey mouthed as Cam listened to Brooke once more. Cam shook his head.

"I love you too. See you this afternoon." Cam hung up, his eyes showing the confusion he felt.

"What's going on?"

"I don't know what it is about the Sinclairs and moving vehicles." He set his empty cup down. "Brooke was sideswiped by a motorcycle last night on her way home from dinner."

"Is she all right? Is her car damaged?"

"She wasn't in her car—she was on foot. She'd just left a coffee shop where'd she met with another student."

Lainey gasped, then waited for Cam to continue.

"The guy who clipped Brooke whisked her away to the hospital and stayed until they checked her out. When they released her, a group of guys, all in suits escorted her outside and into a waiting car. They're taking her someplace to question her about what she saw just before the accident, and about her boyfriend."

Lainey narrowed her eyes at Cam. "Boyfriend? I didn't think she had a boyfriend."

Shit, Cam thought as the conversation played back in his mind. "Neither did I. The guy she met with is the son of some drug lord in Mexico. The guy who hit her with his motorcycle is a fed. They think Brooke is the kid's girlfriend..."

*****

Join me in the continuation of the MacLarens of Fire Mountain Contemporary series with All Your Nights, Book Four

He lives on the edge...She's strictly by the book. Start reading All Your Nights today!

If you want to keep current on all my preorders, new releases, and other happenings, sign up for my newsletter: https://www.shirleendavies.com/contact-me.html

A Note from Shirleen

Thank you for taking the time to read **One More Day**!

If you enjoyed it, please consider telling your friends or posting a short review. Word of mouth is an author's best friend and much appreciated.

I care about quality, so if you find something in error, please contact me via email at shirleen@shirleendavies.com

Books by Shirleen Davies

Contemporary Western Romance Series

MacLarens of Fire Mountain

Second Summer, Book One
Hard Landing, Book Two
One More Day, Book Three
All Your Nights, Book Four
Always Love You, Book Five
Hearts Don't Lie, Book Six
No Getting Over You, Book Seven
'Til the Sun Comes Up, Book Eight
Foolish Heart, Book Nine

Macklins of Whiskey Bend

Thorn, Book One
Del, Book Two
Boone, Book Three

Historical Western Romance Series
Redemption Mountain

Redemption's Edge, Book One
Wildfire Creek, Book Two
Sunrise Ridge, Book Three

Dixie Moon, Book Four
Survivor Pass, Book Five
Promise Trail, Book Six
Deep River, Book Seven
Courage Canyon, Book Eight
Forsaken Falls, Book Nine
Solitude Gorge, Book Ten
Rogue Rapids, Book Eleven
Angel Peak, Book Twelve
Restless Wind, Book Thirteen
Storm Summit, Book Fourteen
Mystery Mesa, Book Fifteen
Thunder Valley, Book Sixteen
A Very Splendor Christmas, Holiday Novella, Book Seventeen
Paradise Point, Book Eighteen,
Silent Sunset, Book Nineteen
Rocky Basin, Book Twenty, Coming Next in the Series!

MacLarens of Fire Mountain

Tougher than the Rest, Book One
Faster than the Rest, Book Two
Harder than the Rest, Book Three
Stronger than the Rest, Book Four
Deadlier than the Rest, Book Five
Wilder than the Rest, Book Six

MacLarens of Boundary Mountain

Colin's Quest, Book One,
Brodie's Gamble, Book Two
Quinn's Honor, Book Three
Sam's Legacy, Book Four
Heather's Choice, Book Five
Nate's Destiny, Book Six
Blaine's Wager, Book Seven
Fletcher's Pride, Book Eight
Bay's Desire, Book Nine
Cam's Hope, Book Ten

Romantic Suspense

Eternal Brethren, Military Romantic Suspense

Steadfast, Book One
Shattered, Book Two
Haunted, Book Three
Untamed, Book Four
Devoted, Book Five
Faithful, Book Six
Exposed, Book Seven
Undaunted, Book Eight
Resolute, Book Nine
Unspoken, Book Ten
Defiant, Book Eleven, Coming Next in the Series!

Peregrine Bay, Romantic Suspense

Reclaiming Love, Book One
Our Kind of Love, Book Two
Edge of Love, Book Three, Coming Next in the Series!
Find all of my books at:
https://www.shirleendavies.com/books.html

About Shirleen

Shirleen Davies writes romance—historical, contemporary, and romantic suspense. She grew up in Southern California, attended Oregon State University, and has degrees from San Diego State University and the University of Maryland. Her passion is writing emotionally charged stories of flawed people who find redemption through love and acceptance. She now lives with her husband in a beautiful town in northern Arizona.

I love to hear from my readers!

Send me an email: shirleen@shirleendavies.com
Visit my Website: https://www.shirleendavies.com/
Sign up to be notified of New Releases:
https://www.shirleendavies.com/contact/
Follow me on Amazon:
http://www.amazon.com/author/shirleendavies
Follow me on BookBub:
https://www.bookbub.com/authors/shirleen-davies

Other ways to connect with me:

Facebook Author Page:
http://www.facebook.com/shirleendaviesauthor
Twitter: www.twitter.com/shirleendavies
Pinterest: http://pinterest.com/shirleendavies
Instagram:
https://www.instagram.com/shirleendavies_author/

Copyright © 2014 by Shirleen Davies

For permission requests, contact the publisher.

Avalanche Ranch Press, LLC
PO Box 12618
Prescott, AZ 86304

Made in the USA
Monee, IL
18 December 2023

49686147R00115